Fourth Down with Everything to Lose

Julie & Mitch Kelly

Copyright © 2015 Julie & Mitch Kelly
All rights reserved.
ISBN: 150850038X
ISBN-13: 9781508500384

DEDICATION

To our extended family at True Life Christian Church.
Thank you for laughing, crying, and celebrating
the love of Jesus alongside us over the last few years.

And, to our family. Thank you for supporting
our dreams and loving us.

TABLE OF CONTENTS

INTRODUCTION 6

CHAPTER ONE 15

CHAPTER TWO 38

CHAPTER THREE 70

CHAPTER FOUR 89

CHAPTER FIVE 109

CHAPTER SIX 123

CHAPTER SEVEN 143

CHAPTER EIGHT 159

CHAPTER NINE 173

CHAPTER TEN 178

EPILOGUE 200

INTRODUCTION

Emma found herself standing in front of an open doorway. She peeked into the room and blinked her eyes several times. The room was beautiful. Even though she was certain she had never been in this room before, she felt an overwhelming sense of warmth wrap around her body like a thick, fleece blanket on a cold night.

Her gaze travelled around the room drinking in the décor. The walls were at least fourteen feet high. Wood beams stretched across the ceiling. Three of the four walls were covered from the floor all the way to the ceiling with ornamental bookcases. The shelves were a dark, rich oak filled with books of all shapes and sizes. The only wall not covered with bookshelves had red floor to ceiling drapes so dark they almost looked black.

Emma bit her bottom lip. Her eyes darted around in an attempt to take in all the features of the room. Clusters of chairs covered in various fabrics and leathers were placed in groups of two or three around the room.

A stone fireplace sat nestled in the corner. Fire leapt from the logs in flashes of blue, white, yellow, and orange as they snapped to a rhythm all their own.

The glare of the flames made it difficult to see. Emma squinted and peered further into the room. There appeared to be someone sitting by the fireplace. Her heart did a funny lurch in her chest. She wasn't alone.

"Emma! Come on in." A warm, masculine voice called out from beside the fireplace. "It's so good to see you!"

Emma hesitated for several seconds but curiosity won out over her fear. She stepped cautiously into the room. Her voice cracked as she asked, "Where am I? Do I know you?" She cringed as a dull pain throbbed in time to her pulse. She lifted her hand and rubbed her temple to ease the pain. She felt like she did when she'd had that nasty sinus infection last year. Her head pounded and she felt oddly disoriented.

The sound of the voice broke into her thoughts. "We haven't met face to face, but yes, you know me. Come in and have a seat."

"Am I dreaming?" Emma said softly.

Sensing her uncertainty, he held out his hand. "No you aren't dreaming. Please, don't be afraid."

Emma walked slowly toward him. As she drew closer his features started to come into focus. Even though he was sitting down, she could tell he was tall. He had broad shoulders, short, dark wavy hair, and a trim, clean beard. She stopped in front of him. His eyes were incredibly warm. They glittered in the firelight like chocolate colored diamonds. She sank down on the ottoman in front of him.

"Where am I? This place is incredible. It's so beautiful."

He smiled. "Thank you. I love this room. I spend a lot of time here." He watched her for a few seconds before he spoke again. This time his voice was softer, "Do you remember anything before standing in the doorway?"

Emma shook her head. "No, I don't remember. When I try to think about how I got here, the pain in my head gets worse." She broke eye contact and looked around the room again. A thought began to form in her mind. She drew in a deep, ragged breath, "Am I dead? I don't feel like I'm awake but if you said I'm not dreaming, does that mean I'm dead?"

"No, Emma, you aren't dead, but you need to remember what happened so we can talk about what to do next." He leaned forward, "Why don't you close your eyes and try one more time to remember where you were before you found yourself standing in my doorway."

Emma nodded slightly and closed her eyes. The throbbing in her head caused her to wince. She drew in another deep breath and tried to fight through the pain. Small snippets slowly started to come to her.

"I remember babysitting the Connor boys. They had just finished all of their homework and had turned on a T.V. show when their dad came home. I remember, he walked me out to my bike, gave me a twenty dollar bill, and waved good-bye as I pedaled down the driveway."

A face flashed before her eyes. Her hand flew to her mouth and her eyes snapped open. She whispered, "Ethan Morgan."

He leaned forward and propped his elbows on his knees. "Good. Now what? What happened next?"

She closed her eyes again and immediately felt fear as she remembered what happened. "I was riding on the side of 122 when Ethan Morgan, one of my classmates, came barreling around the corner in his truck. When he saw me, he started to swerve toward me. He swerved toward me a couple of times. I remember I tried to hold on to the handlebars of my bike, but I was getting really scared. I could barely stay upright. My bike was wobbling all over the place. He swerved toward me again, but this time, he lost control of his truck and I lost control of my bike. The smell of burning rubber was overwhelming. That's the last thing…" Emma's eyes popped open wide. "He ran me off the road didn't he?"

"Yes. He ran you off the road and caused you to wreck your bike." The man nodded, gently confirming her recollection.

"I don't understand. You said I'm not dreaming or dead." She looked down at her body and ran her hands up and down her legs and arms. "Something is off. I don't know how to describe it except to compare it to how I feel when I have the flu and I'm running a fever. I feel slightly out of it, hot, and exhausted. What's going on? Who are you?" Tears filled her eyes, "Please. Tell me what's happening."

He reached over and put his hand on her knee. "Relax Emma, its okay. I've got you." His touch sent a warm current through her entire body. She felt the tension in her body fade away and the pain in her head let up. He gave her a sad smile. "You are not dead. When you wrecked your bike, you flew over the handlebars and hit your head really hard."

"Am I going to die?"

"I'm not sure. It depends. Do you want to die?"

"I don't know. I'm not scared of dying."

"Why not?"

She shrugged, "I know where I'm going when I die."

"Why is that?"

"Because I serve Jesus. He's my savior."

"That's awesome Emma." A big smile spread over the man's face.

She smiled back at him, happy he'd agreed with her. The smile slowly slipped off of her face as she thought about what it would mean if she died. She looked at the fire as tears filled her eyes.

"What's wrong?"

"I don't think I'm ready to die yet. There's a lot of work left to do. I know God could find someone else to do it if I died, but, I don't know, I just feel like there are people I could still reach. People like... Ethan Morgan."

"The kid that put you here? What's he got to do with it?" The man sounded surprised.

Emma clenched her hands in front of her stomach. "He wasn't always full of hate and anger. We used to be close. We went to church together, played together. Ten years ago everything changed."

"Emma, he ran into you with a two thousand pound truck. That is not the definition of a friend. I'd say things changed a lot."

"I know. I think that's part of the problem. He's forgotten how to be a friend. He's been angry for so long. He's lost his way."

"Emma, his future is not a pretty one if he doesn't make some major changes. He's hurt a lot of people."

Emma blew out a breath strong enough to move her bangs. "I know. I don't want that for him."

He stood to his feet, grabbed the poker for the fireplace, and started to rearrange the logs. "I don't know Emma. You don't owe him anything." He glanced over at her, "Just say the word and we could leave this place right now. I know a couple of folks who would love to meet you face to face."

Emma looked at him, then at the fire, and back at him again. Her eyes slowly widened in surprise as she figured out who she was talking to. For several seconds all she could do was stare at Him.

He put the poker back and sat on the edge of the chair. His eyes searched hers, "I came to bring you home."

"So I'm going to die?"

"Not necessarily." He rubbed his hands together and then held them out to her. She drew in a shaky breath and slipped her hands in His. A surge of warmth spread throughout her body. She closed her eyes and felt the pain in her head subside until it was gone completely.

His voice was softer when He spoke. "Emma, you are in a coma. A limbo between life and death. Not many people get to experience this limbo. You don't truly belong to one place or the other. What would you do if you had five days to move around however you chose?"

Emma tried to process what He was saying. Her head didn't hurt anymore, but her mind was so overwhelmed that she had to repeat to herself exactly what He had said and as she did, a smile formed on her lips and spread over her face. She lifted her eyes to His, "I would make it a week that Ethan Morgan would never forget."

"Are you sure?"

She nodded.

He sighed, "You've witnessed to him over the years and he's been extremely adamant about not believing, but stranger things have happened, so if it's what you want…"

Her face lit up. "Thank you!" She jumped to her feet and threw her arms around His neck and hugged Him tight.

He kissed her cheek and set her back on her feet in front of Him so He could look in her eyes. "I'll see you in a week."

CHAPTER ONE

"Come on, Ethan, get your act together!" Coach screamed at me from the sidelines. Wiped out from hours of practice and frustrated with my less than stellar performance, I pulled back my arm and launched the ball in a perfect spiral.

I held my breath and watched as the ball sailed high above my wide receiver's hands. He leaped high in the air to try and catch it; instead, he came down empty handed. My shoulders slumped. I yanked my helmet off and stomped toward the sideline.

Coach threw his playbook down and pointed his finger at me. "That's it! Everybody, ten laps! While you're running, you can contemplate if football is really the sport for you and you can personally thank Ethan for a grueling end to a grueling day."

His face was a nice shade of purple as he finished his rant. "Now, get running before I make it fifteen!"

I turned away from him, threw my helmet down beside the bench, and started jogging down the sideline. The other guys fell in beside me. I glared at Tommy, my wide receiver. "You could've jumped a little higher."

"Dude, I could've been three feet taller and still wouldn't have caught that ball. What's up with you today?"

I snapped at him, "What's up with me? What about you? Only losers make excuses." I sped up and pulled ahead of the group. I wasn't in the mood to listen to them whine like Kindergartners.

As I rounded the field and jogged by the bench, coach yelled out, "Scouts aren't gonna be impressed with overthrown balls and missed plays Morgan. Get your head in the game!"

I resisted the urge to flip him off or say something that would get me benched, but oh, how I wanted to. I had scouts from every major college in the area coming to see me play this season. So far, even Ohio State and Michigan had made appearances at my games. Did coach really think I didn't know how important every single play of every game was?

With each lap I ran my anger surged.

When I finished my laps, I stormed over to my truck, threw my football gear in the back, opened the door, and slid behind the wheel. I started the truck, threw it in reverse, and laughed as I sprayed gravel all over everyone else's cars leaving the parking lot.

....

I tore through our little town. Like a lot of small towns, Oakdale rolls up its sidewalks when it gets dark. A few cars were parked in the grocery store parking lot, but otherwise the streets were empty.

I made my way out of what little there is of downtown and turned onto route 122. I took a deep breath, I needed time to clear my head, and it wasn't like Dad would be waiting at home to hear about my day, so I decided to take the scenic way home.

I tapped my fingers against the steering wheel in time to the song on the radio. The pounding of the drums and the screech of the guitars suited my mood. I thought about stopping at Ava's on my way home.

I glanced at myself in the rearview mirror. My face was sweaty and smudged with dirt from practice and my hair was all messed up. I resembled a blonde labradoodle that had been left out in the rain. My girlfriend probably wouldn't appreciate it if I showed up at her house smelling like a locker room. I ran my hand through my hair and decided against the impromptu visit. I'd see her at school in the morning.

I drove around one of the many bends on 122 and noticed a flash of light ahead. As I got closer I could tell it was the reflector on a bike. I eased my foot off the gas pedal and slowed down to see if I recognized the rider, it was a face I'd know anywhere. Emma Montgomery. I've known her forever.

She's been sitting in front of me in almost every class since Kindergarten. A long time ago, we were even friends. I rolled my eyes. Why I was ever friends with such a weirdo was beyond me. She's cute enough in a girl next door kind of way. There are times she reminds me of the actress Katie Holmes. What I can't stand is her holy-roller attitude. She's into church and Jesus and all that corny religious garbage. It makes me want to puke.

I slowed my truck down even further and let her catch back up with me. When she glanced in the passenger side window, I gave her my best sarcastic smile. Her bike wobbled as she swerved over onto the gravel at the edge of the road. I felt a surge of adrenaline as I watched her struggle.

I laughed out loud at her clumsy attempt to gain control of her bike. I let off the gas again and waited for her to catch up. I teasingly swerved my truck toward her bike. I heard her yelp as she swerved onto the gravel and watched her try to pull further away from me. This was too easy.

The third time, I let off the gas and slowed down again and let her ride past me. I pulled my truck directly behind her and revved the engine really loud.

After that, I'm not completely sure what happened. Everything happened so fast. Her bike started to fishtail. I hit the brakes. She lost control of her bike and swerved toward the guardrail. When the front wheel of her bike slammed into the guardrail, it sent her sailing over the handlebars. My truck screeched to a stop as I watched her get sucked into the night, over the embankment. I threw the door of my truck open, jumped out, and yelled, "Emma!"

She was gone. All I could see was her bike twisted and broken, lying against the guardrail with the front wheel still spinning.

....

My fingers drummed against the table in an agitated rhythm as I fidgeted in the torture device they called a chair. I looked around the room. There wasn't a lot to see. Four light blue walls surrounded me. The table in front of me was stainless steel. The only way out of the room was through a gray steel door. The mirror that stretched across the wall beside me had to be a two way mirror. I could feel at least one person watching me, maybe several people.

I rubbed my arms. The room apparently didn't have any heat. I pulled my jacket around me and drew in a deep breath. Somehow the night had gotten totally out of control. Whenever I closed my eyes, I could see Emma going over the handlebars of her bike and disappearing into the dark. I shifted in my chair as an uncomfortable feeling washed over me.

I leaned my elbows on the table and rubbed my eyes. After she had gone over the handle bars, I called out to her so many times I lost count. I'd fumbled around the truck for my cell phone and called 911. When the paramedics arrived they found her lying unconscious down an embankment on the side of the road. If she'd gone a couple more feet she would've landed in the creek.

I closed my eyes and I could see the paramedics in my mind. The red flashing lights, the chaos of the search, the yelling when they found her. I watched off to the side as they knelt beside her on the ground and flooded the area with lights.

They didn't waste any time getting to work on her. One of the paramedics grabbed a blue bag and held it to her mouth. He held it over her mouth and squeezed it every couple of seconds. A second paramedic secured a brace around her neck and listened to her heart and checked her eyes with a slim light. I couldn't hear everything they were saying. I caught glimpses like, "don't move her to fast..." "We don't... choice...not breathing....own".

Finally, when they had her secured on a flat board, they all counted to three and heaved her up onto a stretcher. Then they raced past me and loaded her into the back of the ambulance.

My heart slammed against my ribs and my eyes flew open as I realized the entire time they worked on her, I never saw her move once.

Once the ambulance had left the scene with sirens blaring, the focus shifted to me. The police asked me to come to the station to answer questions. I hadn't been given much of a choice so I agreed.

I flopped back in the chair. I tried to push the images of Emma lying on the ground out of my mind. I shifted my focus to my current situation. Since I'd arrived at the police station, I'd only talked to a female officer named Diaz. She'd taken a brief statement, given me a cup of water, and left me alone in the interview room.

What was taking so long? Why was I still stuck in this room? I didn't have a watch or my cell phone so I had no idea how long I'd been stuck in this blue room waiting but it had to have been a long time. It sure felt like forever. What if they knew what I had done? Did they know I'd been tormenting Emma before hitting her?

I couldn't help myself, I bolted out of the chair and started to pace. I couldn't sit in that chair one more minute. Just as panic set in and my nerves threatened to overwhelm me, the door opened and Officer Diaz stepped into the room.

My dad walked in behind her. My eyes flew open wide at the sight of him. He did not look happy as he stood in the doorway. His hair was messed up and his clothes were wrinkled. It was evident he'd either been asleep or close to it when he found out about the accident.

Officer Diaz motioned the chairs and said, "Why don't we have a seat Ethan."

I dutifully crossed the room and sank back down onto the chair. Office Diaz sat down across from me. My dad remained standing. His eyes drilled holes in the side of my face. I gulped and looked down at my hands.

"Hey, Ethan. Sorry about the wait." Office Diaz said as placed a notebook and pen on the table. "Things have been a little crazy. You doing okay? Can I get you anything?"

I shook my head no and pulled my focus off of my dad and back to her. I knew by the pit in my stomach that my dad would have more to say later. Probably a lot more. "I'm okay. Has there been any news on Emma? Is she okay?"

Officer Diaz shook her head no, "She's pretty banged up. The doctors at the hospital are doing the best they can to save her." She leaned forward and opened the notebook. Rifling through it, she found a blank page. Her eyes shifted back to me, "I know we went over what happened, but I have some questions. Now that your dad's here, we can get started."

"I'll answer whatever I can."

She smiled at me, "Great. Will you go through what happened tonight? Tell me again what you saw?"

I paused for several seconds. While I'd been waiting in this tiny room, I had been given plenty of time to get my story together. Now I had to sell it to her and my dad. No one could know about what I'd done, how it was my fault Emma was fighting for her life. My football career depended on it. My life depended on it. Maybe Emma wouldn't even remember the accident. I'd have to figure out a way to deal with her when she woke up. If she didn't remember what happened, I sure wasn't going to tell her. If she did remember, I would reason with her and if that didn't work, then I would threaten her. I just had to stick to my version of what had happened.

Fourth Down with Everything to Lose

I clasped my hands together and laid them on the table. I leaned forward and spoke quietly, "I left football practice at the high school football field around 8:00p.m. I drove through town and then out state route 122 to go home. I live outside town on Geary road. I was listening to music and thinking about going to see my girlfriend. I drove around the corner, the one just past Harper Drive, when I saw a flash of light ahead of me. My first thought was that it was a dog or a deer, but as I got closer I could tell it was a bike of some kind so I tried to slow down. I think I accidentally hit the gas instead of the brake. The noise must have frightened Emma because she jerked the handlebars of the bike and swerved toward the truck. I slammed on the brakes but it didn't help. She lost control of the bike. She clipped the front of my truck and then she swerved back to the side of the road and ran into the guardrail. When her bike made contact she flipped over the handlebars. I couldn't see where she landed. I got out of my truck and called out to her. She didn't answer so I called 911."

Officer Diaz crossed her arms, "Why did you go home that way?? State route 122 is dangerous. There are a lot of curves and dips. Isn't there a safer route?"

I shrugged, glanced at my dad, and then looked down at the table. "I was aggravated and needed to clear my head. I thought 122 would be enough of a drive to help me cool off."

"Were you drinking or had you taken drugs?"

"No!" I exclaimed and looked up directly into her eyes, "In fact, I volunteered for a Breathalyzer at the scene. I don't have anything to hide."

"Why were you so upset?"

"I wasn't hitting my marks at practice. I kept overthrowing my wide receivers. Coach was on my case about it. He made us all run laps after practice."

"I see. Do you have to run extra laps a lot?"

I rolled my eyes. "Hardly. I was just having an off night."

"How well do you know Emma Montgomery?"

"Not very well. We used to be friends when we were little but for the past ten years we've barely spoken."

"Why is that?"

"We don't hang out with the same people."

"Oh?"

I shrugged. "I'm a football player. She's kind of nerdy. We don't have anything in common."

Officer Diaz sighed and sat back in her chair watching me. When she spoke her voice was compassionate. "Ethan, I'm sorry this happened to you and Emma. I think it was just a case of her being in the wrong place at the wrong time. From the information I've been able to gather it seems like an accident. Until Emma wakes up and gives us her statement, we are going to rule it an accident. We won't be filing any charges at this time. Is there anything else you want to add before we let you out of here?"

Relief flooded my body. I pulled my hands off the table and ran them through my hair. I drew in a deep breath and said, "I really hope she'll be okay."

"She's young and strong and the doctors are working very hard to give her a fighting chance. She's lucky you had a phone and were able to call 911 so fast."

She stood up. "We'll be in touch if we have any additional questions."

I stood up and nodded my head, "Whatever I can do to help officer."

She opened the door and motioned me to follow her out into the hallway. As I walked by her, she gently patted my back, "We need more courageous young people like you Ethan."

Her words felt like little knives under my skin. The accident hadn't been nearly as innocent as I made it sound. What would happen when Emma woke up?

I took a deep breath, shook it off, and walked out into the hall way. I would deal with Emma when she woke up. I just needed a plan.

....

As we walked out of the police station, Dad stopped and held his hand out palm up for my keys. He didn't say a single word, but I knew better than to try and argue with him. So I plopped them in his hand with no argument. I climbed in the passenger side and promptly leaned my head against the window.

The roar of the engine was the only thing that broke the quiet inside the cab. I watched the town disappear out of sight for the second time that night as we headed home.

I knew better than to be the first one to speak. My dad's face had stayed the same shade of red as when he had entered the interview room at the police station. No words were necessary for me to know how upset he was with me. His look said it all.

I knew it was just a matter of time before the explosion.

He jerked the truck into the driveway and came to a stop beside the house. I didn't wait for him to shut the engine off, I opened the door, climbed out of the truck, and hustled to the back door. Thankfully in his rush to get to the police station, he'd left the kitchen door unlocked. I almost made it through the kitchen before something smacked me in the back of the head.

"What is the matter with you? Is it too hard to just go to school, play football and get good grades? What in the hell were you doing out on 122 after dark on a school night? How many times have I told you not to go that way?"

I rubbed my head where he hit me with the rolled up newspaper he must have picked up off the table. I fumbled to find the right words, "Dad, I…"

He cut me off mid-sentence. "I don't want to hear your lame excuses!" He threw his hands up in the air, "Why can't you do what I tell you? Are you stupid? What do you think I do, talk to hear myself talk? You could have killed that girl and then what? Your football career would be over. Done. Finished before it even started. There are college scouts coming to your games this year. You can't be in juvenile detention or labeled a trouble maker before you even get to college."

He jerked open the refrigerator door, grabbed a beer, and slammed the door shut. I leaned against the corner of the cabinet by the door. There was no slinking off while he was on a roll. I'd have to try and wait it out.

He cracked open the beer, took a big gulp and slammed it on the table. "I work two jobs so you can play football, have nice clothes, and drive a decent truck. Is it asking too much to expect you to stay out of trouble?" He paused for a couple of seconds, his hands gripping the back of one of the kitchen chairs so tightly his knuckles turned white.

He blew out a huge breath of air and continued, "You need to wake up kid. Life is full of opportunities to make the wrong choices. You have to think about your future." His shoulders slumped, "You don't want to end up working in a factory like me. You have a real chance to do something with your life. Don't blow it being stupid."

He picked up the beer can and stormed by me, out of the kitchen, down the hall, and into his den. I winced as the door slammed. It would be useless to follow him. Once he went in the den that was it for the night. He might come out for another beer, but it definitely wouldn't be to talk to me.

I walked down the hall and went up the stairs. I shut the door, kicked off my shoes, and walked over to the window that looks out into the yard. My mind was spinning. I couldn't get the image of Emma flipping over the handlebars out of my mind. Why couldn't she control her bike? Why did she have to freak out and wreck? I should've gone home the normal route. I had no business on 122 and I definitely had no business tormenting Emma as she tried to get home.

I turned away from the window and scooped up a small basketball and squeezed it. I squeezed it until it made my hands hurt. Anger surged through me. I threw the ball and felt brief flash of satisfaction as it slammed against the headboard of my bed and then bounced to the floor.

I trudged to the bed and sank down. Exhaustion rolled over me. I kicked my shoes off and flopped back. My entire body ached and my mind felt heavy.

As I laid there, my stomach growled. The last thing I'd eaten was a hamburger at lunch and that had been hours ago. I closed my eyes, no way was I going back downstairs.

I was almost asleep when my cell phone buzzed. I snatched it out of my pocket and glared at the screen. It was Ava. She'd sent me a text.

"U ok?"

I rolled my eyes and muttered, "Just peachy." But instead I texted, "Yeah, tired but ok."

"People are talking, what happened? How is Emma?"

Great, the whole school probably already knew. I typed, "I don't know. She was in bad shape when they took her to the hospital."

"Wow! That sucks. Hope she'll be okay. U need anything?"

"No. Tired. Need sleep."

"Ok."

"See u tomorrow"

"Lov…" I clicked the screensaver button and tossed the phone on the nightstand. I put my arm over my eyes. Tomorrow was going to suck. Everyone would be running around talking about the accident. Emma would be in her element, damsel in distress and all that crap. Hopefully in a day or two everyone would move on to the next crisis.

As I drifted off to sleep I found myself wishing that for once my dad would've been more concerned about me than my football career. But as usual, he never even asked if I was okay. For all he knew I could've been hurt too. He hadn't always been so distant and cold. When I was little I would sit on his lap and help him drive the lawnmower or I would follow him around the house as he fixed things. We were inseparable. He changed so much when mom died.

....

Sometime later in the night, something jostled my bed. My eyes popped open. I propped myself up on my elbow to see what had touched my bed. The light of my alarm clock cast a green glow across the room and illuminated a figure standing at the end of my bed.

I blinked a couple of times. The figure was still there. I squinted, it was Emma. Every nerve ending in my body jerked. I jumped backward and banged my head against the headboard of my bed.

She took a step toward me. I held up my hand. "Whoa! What are you doing here?" I moved my hand to rub the spot on my head that had hit the headboard.

She stopped and stared at me. I blinked a few more times trying to focus. My brain felt sluggish with sleep. I drew in a ragged breath and stared blankly at her for a minute in complete disbelief.

The air around her shimmered. It reminded me of a corn field on a hot, humid August afternoon. She was enveloped in a mist that made seeing her clearly difficult.

"How did you get here? What are you doing in my room?" I snapped. Maybe she'd gotten out of the hospital, or maybe this was because I went to bed on an empty stomach.

"I came to warn you."

"Warn me about what?" I asked confused. "Couldn't you have waited until we were at school later?"

She propped her hand on her hip. "That's going to be a little difficult considering I'm in the hospital."

"No you're not. You're standing right here. I can see you."

She held her hands up and looked down at them as she turned them over and then back up. She thrust them toward me, "Is this how I normally look?"

"No. actually, you look kind of weird." I squinted at her, "You almost look... faded."

"Yeah, I can see that." She sighed.

I looked at her for a minute and it suddenly occurred to me how odd it was that one, she was in my room at all, and two, that I couldn't quite bring her into focus. A thought came to me and I blurted out. "Are you a ghost?"

"No. I'm not a ghost."

"I don't get it. What's going on?" I was getting confused.

She sighed and sank down on the bed by my feet. She turned her body to face me. "I came to talk to you Ethan."

"About what?" I snorted. "We're not exactly friends." I fidgeted until my back rested against the headboard with my legs crossed in front of me.

She rolled her eyes. "I came to ask you to homecoming." She snorted, "Not. I came to talk about what happened tonight. You know, how you ran me off the road and tried to kill me?"

"I didn't try to kill you!"

"Really?"

"Really. Anyway, you seem fine now." I waved my hand at her.

"Am I?" She swept her hand down the front of her body.

I couldn't argue with that. She definitely didn't look alright. Her eyes were the same chocolate brown, her hair was the same wavy brown but she wasn't.... solid. I reached over and tried to grab her arm. Instead of touching her shirt, my hand went right through her. I jerked my hand back, "What the... you are dead!"

"No I'm not dead. I'm in a coma." She crossed her arms, "The coma you put me in. Did you really think that I would magically be okay after what happened? And, the first place I would go, would be here, to see you?"

I couldn't speak. This wasn't possible. If she wasn't a ghost, how was she here at all? I reached down and pinched my arm…

hard. Yelping, I rubbed my arm and looked back toward where she was sitting. She was still there staring at me.

She cocked her head to the side, "It's not a dream genius. I'm really here."

Okay, it wasn't a dream either. I was speechless. I stuttered, "How? Why? What's... going on?"

Emma uncrossed her arms and leaned forward. "I'm here to see if there is a chance for you."

"A chance? For me?" I snorted.

"Yep."

"A chance for what? It's not my fault that you can't ride a bike or take a little teasing."

"Seriously?" she snapped. "That's your response? You terrorize me and put me in the hospital and it's my fault?" She looked up at the ceiling and yelled, "You may be right, this could be a lost cause."

I looked up, "Who are you talking to?"

She sighed and gave me a long stare. "Are you really okay with what you did?"

I started to get angry, really angry. "I don't know what this is all about but I'm not interested. You can take your sad face and heavy sighs and go make someone else feel guilty. You lost control of your bike. End of story."

Emma stood up beside my bed, took a couple of steps toward me, and put her hands on her hips and leaned toward me, "Ethan, you've got one shot. Got it? One shot to change your life and stop what's coming if you don't. God gave me a chance to visit you and help you see what a mess you're making of things."

"Awesome. Here comes the God crap. Why do you even care? If you are in a coma and can travel anywhere you want, wouldn't you rather visit your family?"

"Because, if I don't reach you in the next few days, it may be too late. I'm not going to let that happen."

"Give me a break. I didn't need your religious hocus-pocus when you were alive and I don't need it now that you're…" I stopped cold. I had been about to say…

"Dead? Were you going to say dead??"

I looked away from her. "I don't need the God loves you speech. I don't want to hear it!"

"I'll be back. You can count on it. This isn't over. I know there's a heart in there somewhere. You can act mean and tough and blow a lot of hot air, but Ethan Morgan, I know you. I'm fighting for you and despite what others have said I believe you can be saved. Get ready to lose some sleep over the next few days. I'm going to show you how your actions could lead to serious consequences. I hope for your sake Ethan that you can be reached. I'll be back. In the meantime, try not to put anyone else in the hospital."

I turned my head back toward her to say something nasty, but she was gone. I was alone in my room. Running my hand through my hair, I wondered what in the world had just happened.

CHAPTER TWO

I swung my truck wide and pulled into my usual spot in the school parking lot. I turned the engine off and leaned my head back against the seat. My eyes drifted closed as I tried to get my bearings. My eyes throbbed from lack of sleep and my body ached as if I had the flu. Even after a super-hot shower, I still felt exhausted and out of sorts.

Between the accident, my dad's rant, and the surprise visit from Emma, "Whatever that was", I hadn't been able to fall back to sleep. I'd spent the rest of the night tossing and turning. What a day to feel like crap. One of the biggest games of the year was coming up tonight.

Irritated, I got out of my truck, grabbed my book bag, slammed the door shut, and trudged across the parking lot toward the school. Before I could get half way to the door I was surrounded by people.

My friends and other students crowded around me.

"How's Emma?"

"What happened?"

"Can you play tonight?"

I grinned and held my hands up in surrender. "Whoa. What's with the inquisition?"

Tommy popped his head up over the others, "Dude, we've been worried. You were a no show on Facebook® and Twitter® last night."

"Yeah," Louis slide over to my side and looked up at me with his dopey brown eyes, "We heard about the accident and then it was total silence. What happened?"

I lowered my backpack to the ground and propped it against my knees. My eyes moved over the small crowd that had gathered. Everyone looked up at me expectantly like baby birds waiting on their mama for food.

I shrugged. "I had an accident on the way home last night. I clipped Emma Montgomery's bike when she lost control of it. She hit the guardrail and got pretty banged up."

Ava pushed through the crowd and put her hand on my arm. "Oh, how awful. Ethan, are you okay?"

I reached out, wrapped my arm around her waist, and pulled her close to my side. I breathed in the smell of her shampoo. Her hair was soft and smelled like coconuts. I leaned in and kissed her softly on the lips. "I'm better now."

She pulled back and put her hand on my chest, "Ethan, not here."

I laughed at her discomfort. "Okay, later then." I kissed her one more time for good measure and let her go. She smoothed her shirt and moved away from me to stand by her girlfriends.

"So how's Emma?" Jesse asked.

I pulled my eyes moved away from Ava to look at Jesse. "I don't know. I haven't heard anything."

He folded his arms across his chest and stared right back at me. "How could you hit her? Didn't you see the reflector on her bike?"

I raised my eyebrow. I didn't like the confrontational tone of his voice. "It was an accident. What exactly are you implying, Jesse?"

He stared back at me for several seconds. His face was set in a stern expression as if he had more he wanted to say. After a long pause, he broke eye contact and looked away from me. He huffed out a big breath of air and responded, "Nothing. I'm not suggesting anything. I just don't get how you didn't see her."

I leaned down and picked up my backpack. I looked him up and down, "That's why it's called an accident." I moved away from the group and walked toward the door of the school.

"Maybe she shouldn't ride on the road if she can't operate a simple bicycle." I called back over my shoulder.

....

By third period I was ready to pull my hair out. All anyone could talk about was the accident and Emma.

I walked into study hall and made my way over to a seat by the window. I slid down into the seat and opened my history book. Maybe doing homework would distract me.

The third time I restarted chapter five; I rubbed my eyes and let my mind drift back to the night before. Had Emma really been in my room?

I shook my head to clear the cobwebs. There was no way she'd really been there, that was crazy. She was in the hospital. Maybe the adrenaline rush and lack of sleep after the accident caused me to have a nightmare.

Louis plopped down in the seat beside me and slammed his books dramatically on his desk. I glanced at the teacher. He gave us a dirty look and went back to his crossword puzzle.

Louis leaned dramatically across the aisle and whispered none too quietly, "Hey did you hear about Emma?"

I glared at him. "What about her jerk face? Haven't you had enough gossip for one day?"

"No way." He snorted. "This is the most exciting thing that's happened in Oakdale in like… forever. Don't you want to know the news?"

"Know what, *news*?"

"Dude, she may not make it. Her brain has started to swell. In fact, Stacey said she heard they may have to cut a hole in her skull to relieve the pressure."

Everything suddenly felt really far away as if I were in a tunnel. I could see Louis' lips move as he continued to yammer on about Emma, but even though I was staring at him, his words didn't register.

My thoughts began to build momentum and race round and around in my head. Emma not going to make it? Impossible! Louis' face started to swim in front of my eyes, the edges of my vision began to fade to black. I blinked and stood up. I needed air or I was going to pass out. No way was that happening in study hall. I bolted for the classroom door.

Mr. Donnelly, the unlucky schmuck who had been assigned to babysit us during study hall yelled out as I passed by his desk, "Morgan, get back here, where do you think you're going?"

I yelled back over my shoulder the first thing that came to my head as I kept walking toward the door. "I have to go see Coach." I didn't look back to see if he bought my lie. I just walked out the door and into the hallway.

As I walked down the hall other students called out to me, "Ethan, you okay?"

"Ready for the big game?"

I ignored everyone who tried to get my attention. Didn't they have anything better to do? Why were there always so many people around?

I rounded the corner by the art room and saw that one of the janitor's closet doors was open. I hurried inside the small closet and shut the door. I leaned my back against the door to keep anyone from following me inside. I covered my face with my hands and tried to slow my breathing. As I inhaled the smell of bleach and an unidentifiable funk, I slid slowly down the door, my feet moving out in front of me as I sank to the floor.

My hands shook as I rubbed my closed eyes. Could Emma really be hurt that bad? Had I killed her? My stomach lurched. Up until now, it hadn't felt so real. If she died it would be my fault. I'd done everything I could to shift the blame, but ultimately it was because of me that she was lying in a hospital bed fighting for her life.

I leaned my head against the door and opened my eyes to find Emma seated cross legged in front of me. I jumped. "Geesh, do you have to do that?"

She shrugged a slight smile lifting the corner of her mouth. "I don't know. I kind of enjoy it."

I rolled my eyes. "I bet you do." I sighed. "Am I dreaming again?"

"I don't know."

"Why are you here? Why do you keep showing up?"

"I told you last night that I'd be back. We aren't done yet."

My voice felt heavy as I spoke, "What if I want us to be done? What if I don't want to play along with your so called mission?"

"If there was another way, you can bet I'd do it, but time isn't on our side. I don't have time to be subtle."

"Because your brain is swelling and you might not wake up?"

She pushed her hair out of her face, "Maybe, I don't know for sure if I'm going to get better. All I know is that God gave me five days to change your heart."

"What?"

"God gave me five days to visit you and show you how your actions have affected the people around you. Not just me, but your friends, the kids at school, and all the kids you torment every day. I don't think you realize the effect you've had on the people in our school."

I grunted, "Your nuts. Everybody loves me. So what if I pick on some losers now and then? It'll toughen them up."

"Is that what you really think? Do they love you, or are they afraid of you?"

I closed my eyes and leaned my head back. "You know what? I don't care if they love me or fear me, the end result is the same. They all do what I say, when I say it. I rule this school."

"Wow, you really are arrogant. I've got my work cut out for me."

"Look, I'm sorry I hurt you. Can't that be enough? Can't you just wake up, get better, and leave me alone?"

"I can't do that."

I opened my right eye and peered at her. "I don't know what you want. My life is perfect. I'm the star of the football team, I have a beautiful girlfriend, and I can do anything in this school that I want too."

"That might all be true on the surface but you need to look a little deeper. Not everything is as perfect as you make it out to be."

"Really?"

She stood up and pointed to the door, "Come on I'll show you."

"What?"

She waved her hand at the door, "I said, come on, I'll show you."

"Seriously?"

"Seriously." She moved around me to stand by the door.

"Do I have a choice?"

"Today? No."

Sighing, I scrambled to my feet and looked down at her, "Fine. Let's get this over with already."

She smiled up at me, "Okay tough guy. Let's go."

I followed Emma out into the hall. There were several clusters of students huddled around their lockers talking and laughing. We approached a group of four freshmen boys standing by their lockers. They passed trading cards back and forth to each other.

One of the boys spoke, "Joe, these are awesome. Where did you get them?"

"My brother sent them to me."

"All the way from California?"

"Yep. He found them at a swap meet and thought I would like them."

"They are pretty freaking awesome."

Joe's head bobbed up and down. "I know. A special collector's edition Star Wars set from 1977."

I stepped up to the one they called Joe. "What's up nerd? Forgot your pacifier so you brought trading cards instead?" He didn't react to me at all.

Puzzled, I waved my hand in front of his face. Nothing. He just kept smiling and talking to his friends. I snapped my fingers at the end of his nose. Still nothing.

I looked over at Emma, "He can't see me?"

"Nope and he can't hear you either."

I rolled my eyes. "This is pointless. Why on earth are we in dorkville? What could I possibly learn (I air quoted learn so she'd know how dumb I thought this was) from them?"

"Just wait." Emma folded her arms and leaned against a couple of empty lockers.

What happened next was just too weird. I heard a noise, turned my head, and watched as I walked around the corner and started heading down the hall.

I looked over at Emma in disbelief. What in the world was going on? My mouth must have dropped open because she motioned me to close it. I gulped and closed it, and watched as the other me approached.

He, I, sure did look intense. Mad at the world. He was carrying a black backpack bulging with books slung over his left shoulder, a scowl on his face, and eyes that radiated anger.

When he walked up on the boys going through their cards, he reached out, grabbed the cards, ripped the whole stack in two and tossed them in the air at the boys. As they floated to the ground in pieces, he didn't miss a stride, he shoved the closest one into the lockers and shouted, "Out of the way losers!"

I cringed a little. It had never bothered me when I did something like that, I always thought it was funny, but seeing myself do it, I was a little embarrassed. Without a care or thought for anyone else, I had torn up something not only sentimental, but valuable.

I watched as Joe, the owner of the cards fought back tears. He and his friends scrambled to pick up the pieces.

The tallest boy glared down the hall at me and announced to the group, "Wow, he is such a dick."

"No kidding." Joe mumbled. His face had lost all of its earlier joy. He was fighting tears as he stared down at the torn cards. "I'm never gonna be able to replace these."

The third boy, the one the other me shoved in the lockers, rolled his eyes, "Why does everyone put up with him?"

"He can throw a football."

"Yeah, well someday we'll have the last laugh."

"How's that??"

"Guys like him peak in high school. He'll probably end up working for one of us, go through three wives, have several freak kids, and drink himself into an early grave. Then we'll see who the loser is."

"Come on Joe, we'll find a way to get you a new set of cards. He's not worth it."

The four of them gathered up their stuff, closed their lockers, and headed down the hall to their next class.

I looked over at Emma. I did my best to hide any feelings I was experiencing. "What was the point of that? Who cares if I tore up some stupid cards? They had it coming."

Emma stared hard into my eyes for several long seconds. My hands flexed into fists at my side. She sighed and broke eye contact, "Uh-huh, whatever you say, I saw your face, Ethan." She pushed away from the lockers and motioned down the hall. "Come on, there's something else I want you to see."

She started walking toward the gym. I blew out a heavy sigh and followed her. This had better be good.

....

"Did you see him at practice last night?"

"Yeah, he was all over the place."

"Coach made all of us run laps because he couldn't get the plays right."

"Apparently he can't drive either."

"I can't believe he hit Emma."

"Do you think it was an accident?"

I stood off to the side and listened as my closest friends sat in the bleachers and talked about me. Even my girlfriend, Ava was there. She was sitting awfully close to Jesse and he wasn't trying to get away from her.

I glared at Emma. "Why are we here? You think my closest friends are going to throw me under the bus, say a bunch of stuff to make me sad and change my ways? This is ridiculous." I waived my hands in front of them and hopped back and forth to try to get their attention. "They really can't see or hear me?"

"Nope. No one can see or hear either of us. We are only here to observe."

"Great. Let's watch and listen as they blow your little theory out of the water. They adore me."

Emma rolled her eyes, "If you say so."

I turned back to listen, expecting them to defend me.

Ava shrugged. "I know Emma irritates him, but I don't think he'd hurt her on purpose." I smiled, I knew Ava would defend me.

Jesse shrugged. "I don't know. Remember what he did to that kid who got lost and ended up at our bonfire last fall?"

Grady, one of the wide receivers on the football team piped up, "Yeah, that might have been a little much."

"You think?" Ava rolled her eyes. "He made that poor kid strip down to his underwear then he put his clothes in the fire, and made him walk over a mile back to his house."

The bell rang in the background, my friends packed up their stuff and headed for the doors.

Jesse and Ava stayed behind. Jesse turned to face Ava, his eyes were sad as he spoke quietly so the others wouldn't over hear him. "Then why are you with him Ava? Can't you see what a jerk he is? He treats you awful."

I strode over to where Jesse and Ava were huddle together and shouted, "She's with me because I'm freaking Ethan Morgan, star of the football team, and she's in love with me."

Ava's eyes softened as she looked back at Jesse. "I know. He's a jerk most of the time, but sometimes he's okay." She let her hand rest on Jesse's for a couple of seconds then drew it back.

Her eyes were sad as she said, "We all know what would happen if I ever broke up with him. My life would be over. His ego couldn't handle it. He would never stop tormenting me. Look what he's done to Emma. Back in the day, she was his best friend. If he's made her life miserable think what he'd do to me." She sighed and tried to smile at Jesse who clearly looked miserable. Getting to her feet she whispered against his ear, "We won't be in high school forever."

My mouth fell open again. What was going on? Had Ava really just implied she was only with me because she had to be? Anger coursed through my entire body. I turned on Emma and shouted. "This is all crap! You aren't real. This isn't happening! My friends would never say this kind of BS about me. I don't want to do this anymore." I threw my hands up in her face and screamed as loud as I could, "Get away from me!"

This had to be a nightmare. I needed to wake up. I crossed the floor of the gym as fast as my legs would carry me, I whipped open the door and felt a tingle of satisfaction as it slammed back against the building. Bright light instantly washed over me. I shielded my eyes and took a step outside.

....

When I woke up in janitor's closet the school day was finally coming to an end. The bell rang and I looked at my watch. My eyes flew open wide. Where had the time gone? It was almost last period. Time for the weekly pep rally.

I left the janitor's closet and jogged down the hall to the gym. I stepped inside the small room off to the left of the stage. The guys stood together in a huddle. When I walked in they got quiet. I leaned against the wall and ignored them. I was too tired to make a big deal out of it. Let them think what they wanted.

I could hear the principal as he yelled announcements through a megaphone, then the pep band played their crappy rendition of, "Welcome to the Jungle" and finally Ava started to announce the players. I watched as everyone lined up to hear their named called. As, the quarterback, I'm always the last one called out to the floor.

While I waited to be called, I decided to go see Emma as soon as the pep rally ended and school was out. I needed to see her, then maybe, I could put these crazy dreams or whatever they were behind me.

When my name was called, I put a half smile on my face and jogged into the gymnasium. As I made my way to the center of the basketball court to join my fellow teammates, the entire student body stood to their feet in the stands. They cheered and clapped until every other sound was drowned out and all you could hear was their applause.

I joined my teammates in the middle of the room and waited for the cheering to end. It didn't. It kept going and going. The teachers clapped, even Coach clapped and smiled along with everyone. He never smiles.

I started to get uncomfortable. It dawned on me why they were so excited and amped up. It was because they thought they were cheering for a hero. They were cheering for me. No one had any idea about what had really happened last night.

I thought briefly about grabbing the megaphone and yelling the truth. Would they clap if they knew I'd run her off the road? Would they stand and cheer if they knew I didn't feel much remorse over what I'd done?

Anger washed over me. I shouldn't have to feel guilty. So what, some nerdy girl got hit riding her bike? Tomorrow everyone would move on to something else. It wasn't as if being teased was new to Emma, surely she should've been able to maintain control of her bike.

I drew in a long breath and tried to shake away the cobwebs, I had to focus, like my dad said. Football was my life. I had to protect the dream.

I forced a big smile, shoved aside the guilt that was trying to rear its ugly head, and waved at the crowd. My response made the clapping grow even louder and more intense. If they wanted a hero, who was I to tell them any different?

I looked out over the crowd and my eyes came to rest on a group of kids who weren't clapping. In fact, they weren't even standing. It was the group Emma typically hung around. There were about ten kids all huddled together toward the top of the bleachers. They didn't look happy with what was going on.

My eyes locked on the tallest kid in the group, Danny Phillips. He is a tall, skinny nerd of a guy. Long arms and legs that seem out of proportion to the rest of his body. Thick glasses, braces, and dark red hair. If you asked my girlfriend, she'd call it auburn or chestnut or some other fancy color. Me, I call it red. Danny moved here about two years ago. It's been my mission to toughen him up ever since.

There is something about the way he looks at me that just sends me over the edge. He acts like he knows something I don't. Like he's above me and the rest of the kids here at Oakdale. I don't know why Emma is friends with him. Even as nerdy as she is, she could do better.

Our eyes met. He glared defiantly at me with his arms crossed in front of his chest. Who did he think he was? I made a mental note to find a way to pay him back after the pep rally for his little rebellion. He couldn't be allowed to show such disrespect with his display of disapproval, especially not during a pep rally.

Coach held his hands up and waved for everyone to quiet down. He grabbed a microphone off the edge of the stage and yelled into it. "Alright, alright, that's enough. Quiet down…quiet down everyone." I pulled my eyes away from Danny and turned to listen to Coach.

Gradually the gym fell quiet (as quiet as a room full of 400 students can be) and Coach spoke. "Before we leave today I want to take a couple of minutes and address what happened to one of our students last night." He walked over and draped his arm around my shoulders.

"Most of you already know that Emma Montgomery and Ethan Morgan were involved in an accident last night. Emma was riding her bike home when Ethan came around the corner and startled her, as a result, she lost control of her bike and wrecked. Ethan showed exceptional bravery by staying at the accident site. He called 911 and waited for help to arrive. Emma's in the hospital and listed in critical condition. I know we are all worried about her and we all hope she has a speedy recovery."

Coach took off his ball cap and bowed his head. "Let's have a moment of silence for Emma."

Everyone bowed their head and the gym got really quiet. I bowed my head to but I couldn't stand still. I shifted from one foot to the other. I didn't want to take a minute to reflect on Emma. I just wanted to forget what happened.

After a couple of minutes, Coach raised his head, gave me a strong squeeze then let go and stepped away from me. "Okay, everyone. What do you say we dedicate tonight's game to Emma? Let's go out there and kick some Hornet butt!"

The students burst into cheers and wild applause. Their obvious compassion toward Emma surprised me. Before I could process what it all meant, my buddies and fellow football players surrounded me and hoisted me up on their shoulders. They walked around the gym floor and chanted, "Emma! Emma!"

I did a mental eye roll, could this get any worse? I didn't want to seem like I was indifferent so I pumped my fist in the air and yelled, "For Emma!" as they carried me out of the gym.

....

As soon as the guys put me down I made some lame excuse about having to check in with my dad and left school as fast as I could.

A few minutes later, I sat quietly in my truck in the parking lot of the hospital. I watched as people drove around and looked for the best parking spot. As I watched them come and go, I wondered if they would have an answer for, or understand what I was going through. They all seemed so clueless as they plodded along with the business at hand.

With considerable effort, I drew in a deep breath and blew it out as hard as I could. I was hoping it would clear the cobwebs in my head. I had to snap out of this funk. The game started in a little over 3 hours. I didn't have time to go crazy. Maybe I had hit my head during the accident and didn't remember doing it. Could a concussion cause you to hallucinate or dream about people in comas? Maybe my subconscious was trying to help me sort through what had happened. Hopefully by actually seeing Emma the dreams, or visions, or whatever they were would stop and I could get on with my life. I wondered if she'd woken up yet and if she had, what was she telling everyone?

I looked up at the hospital. The crown jewel of Oakdale. Best technology in the state, at least that's what the television ads all chirped. I barely remember the original building. Throughout the last ten years a lot of new sections have been added. Now it looks like a college campus of mismatched buildings and parking lots. You could tell they had tried to cheer up the grounds with flowers and the buildings with fresh paint, but nothing could hide what it really was, a place where people came to either get over what had sidelined them or, in my mom's case, a place to die.

My hands tightened on the steering wheel. I didn't have to go in. I could turn the key, start my truck, and drive away. My right hand reached for the key. I stopped myself right before I could grip the key. I needed to do this. It was the only way I was going to be able to stop the crazy that was building in my head. I needed to see how bad things really were.

I jerked the keys out of the ignition with my right hand and reached over with my left hand to yank open the door. I slid out of the truck before I could change my mind.

I gave myself a pep talk as I crossed the parking lot. "You can do this. You can walk through those doors and go to Emma's room. You can do this…" I felt like an idiot muttering to myself, but this was so much harder than I expected. All I wanted to do was run the other way.

The doors of the hospital whooshed close behind me. I walked up to the front desk and attempted a smile at the little old lady manning the desk. Her name tag read "Millie". She was hunched over a crossword puzzle. She looked up at me from behind thick glasses. Her lips lifted in a smile, "Can I help you honey?"

"I'm looking for Emma Montgomery."

"Ok, let's see what room she's in. Emma… Montgomery…" She ran her bent thumb down a sheet of paper until she came to the M's. She clicked her thumb against the paper in triumph. "Here we go, Emma Montgomery. She's in the ICU." Her eyes lifted back up to meet mine. They were filled with compassion. "Take the elevator to the 3rd floor, make a left and follow the hall way to the double doors. Use the phone on the wall to call the desk and they will buzz you in."

"Thank you." I muttered.

"You're welcome. The gift shop is over by the cafeteria if you'd like to buy your friend a gift."

I nodded and moved away from the desk. I doubted a gift would be welcome. In fact, I probably wasn't welcome.

The elevator ride was too short. When the door slid open all I wanted to do was hit the button and ride back down and make a run for it. I stepped out in to the hall and turned left like Millie suggested. As I walked down the hall toward the ICU, I was overcome with the sounds and smells. Even though companies spend millions of dollars to make the cleaners smell "friendly" there is no mistaking what they are; germ killers, antiseptics, and alcohol. All things used to help mask the smell of sickness.

I did my best to keep my eyes straight ahead. I remembered how I felt the day my mom died. Every time someone walked by her room, I would look up in hope that it was the doctor or nurse who was going to be able to save her. The one who would have the answer and stop the nightmare. No one like that ever showed up, it was always other families on their way to see loved ones or doctors and nurses rushing from one task to another.

I came to a stop in front of the double doors. I told myself they were just doors. Cold steel doors with a big sign that read, Intensive Care Unit, please dial zero for admittance. I lifted the receiver off of the red phone hanging on the wall, pushed "0", and waited.

"May I help you?"

"Yes. I'm here to see Emma Montgomery."

Pause. "Okay. I'll buzz you in. She's in room 8"

I put my hand on the door handle and paused. I could still turn around and leave. Instead of giving in to the fear, I straightened my shoulders, took a deep breath, and when the buzz sounded I made myself pull the door toward me.

As I stepped in the ICU and started down another hallway I was overwhelmed by the sounds. There were beeps, blips, and alarms all around me. Nurses walked in and out of rooms, curtains were pulled. One of the rooms had the door shut and sign on it that read, Family Only. I looked away and continued down the hall. I rubbed my hands on my jeans and forced down the panic that threatened to swallow me.

Her room was located just off to the side of the nurse's station. One of the nurses was talking on the phone as I passed. She smiled at me. I tried to smile back. I don't think I was very successful. My mouth was so dry it was hard to swallow. My lips felt permanently stuck together. My tongue felt like it was three sizes too big.

When I reached the door, I stopped cold. Emma wasn't in the room alone. Danny was sitting by her bed. My eyes darted from him back to her.

I didn't recognize the girl in the bed. I blinked several times to clear my eyes. Her face was so swollen that her nose was smashed against her cheeks. Her right eye was black and blue and completely swollen shut. She couldn't have opened it if she was awake and trying. A square bandage covered the right side of her head where they had shaved her hair. Blood was slowly seeping through it turning the white bandage an odd shade of brown and red.

A blue tube was coming out of her mouth and led to a machine sitting just behind the head of her bed. Every few seconds it hissed and puffed. I knew that sound. She was on a ventilator.

My lungs felt heavy as I listened to the steady sound of the machine. I wanted to breathe with her as it forced air into her lungs and back out again.

A tiny ray of hope surged through me maybe this wasn't Emma. It sure didn't look like her, maybe she was in another room.

Danny moved and his movement caught my eye. My shoulders slumped. I realized it had to be Emma. He wouldn't be in a stranger's room looking so miserable. Tears filled my eyes. Everything was becoming way too real. Emma didn't look like someone who would simply snap out of it and be okay. She looked…. broken.

Danny moved again. He bowed his head over his clasped hands as they rested on the edge of Emma's bed. His shoulders slumped forward as he rested against the mattress of her bed. Tears streamed down his cheeks. I turned to leave, but his words stopped me. I wanted to hear what he said.

"Dear God, its Danny. I'm with Emma. She's hurt really bad, but you know already know that. She needs a miracle. I know you can make one happen. You heal people all the time. Lord, please heal her, she's my best friend. She's been there for me through a lot of hard times. She loves you so much. God, I need her. She helps me keep my eyes on you and to keep the darkness at bay. There are a lot of people who need her. Lord, I pray in Jesus' name that you will touch her and heal her completely."

I shifted nervously from my left foot to my right. What Danny was saying was crazy. God, if he, or she, or whoever, is even real he isn't listening. He doesn't care about one hurt girl. Everyone is special to someone and everyone is going to die. Mom was special.

Danny's prayer continued. As he spoke I felt the blood drain from my face.

"And Lord, I'm not sure what really happened the other night. I don't know if I believe it was an accident. Only you, Emma, and Ethan know for sure what really happened. I just pray you'll work on Ethan. He needs you in a big way. He's so full of hate and anger. I haven't known him as long as Emma so I don't even know if there's any good in him, she always said there was, but I have my doubts. Anyway, I pray you will put people in his path that will witness to him. He sure won't listen to me, and frankly, I don't want to talk to him. Lord, you know the things he's done. I pray he'll find you before it's too late. Amen"

I bolted. I turned and walked as fast as I could back down the hallway. My face burned. Who did that self-righteous punk think he was? What nerve to pray for me and say I needed God and how awful I was? His words felt like needles being stabbed through my skin.

As I rode the elevator down and walked back out the front entrance, I vowed that somehow I would make him pay for his stupid prayer. I, Ethan Morgan, sure as hell didn't need Danny Phillips praying on my behalf.

·······

When I stormed out of the hospital, I was so angry it made my head throb. He had a lot of nerve. I was almost across the parking lot when I heard my name being called.

"Ethan. Wait up."

I stopped mid stride and turned around in utter disbelief. Danny jogged across the parking lots as he made his way toward me. My hands squeezed into fists. If he wanted a fight he was going to get one. Now was as good a time as any.

Danny stopped in front of me. His breath was ragged from running and his eyes flashed. I'd never seen him look so angry. Typically he did his best to run away from me not run toward me.

"What do you want dimwit?" I snapped.

He drew in another ragged breath and shouted, "What are you doing here? Why would you show your face in her hospital room?" He paused to breathe and then resumed his tirade. "What on earth made you think she or anyone in her family would want you anywhere near her?"

I crossed my arms in front of my chest and lifted my chin to look down at him. "I don't answer to you."

He took me by surprise and pushed his finger into my chest. "When it comes to her, you answer to me and anyone else who cares about her. You sure don't. You've made that clear for years. You never pass up a chance to embarrass her or call her out in front of her friends. You've done your best to make her and everyone she hangs out with miserable. Why would you ever think she'd want you at her bedside? Especially since you're the one who put her there?"

Before he could drop his hand, I grabbed his finger and bent it backward as hard as I could. I smiled when he gasped and his knees started to buckle.

I leaned in close to stare him in the eyes as I continued to twist. I smiled as I said, "You don't get to stand up to me. You don't get to act like you're better than I am. I could end you right now. I could flatten you on this concrete and they'd need a stretcher to get you into the hospital."

"Wow...." He choked out between gasps. "You're a real stud Ethan, always proving how big and bad you are..."

I laughed, "You need to understand where you fall in the pecking order. Who do you think you are? You think you can boycott the pep rally and it wouldn't be noticed or that I wouldn't respond? Haven't you learned anything?"

I increased the pressure again and held on for a few seconds then I let go and shoved him back a few steps. He grabbed his finger and squeezed it. Anger flashed in his eyes.

I waved my hand at him as if he were a fly. "You know what? I'm feeling generous. I won't break your fingers. Today anyway. And, not that it's any of your business, but I came to see if she was okay. I wanted to see for myself how she was doing."

Danny continued to glare at me as he rubbed his finger and regained his composure. "And how was she hot shot? She seem okay to you?" His words stung and his bravado surprised me. He waved his hand at my truck. "How do any of us know you didn't do this on purpose? Maybe you saw her riding home on the side of the road and thought, gee, here's my chance to show her who the boss is?" He clapped his hands together really slowly, "Well congratulations. Well done. You sure showed a hundred pound girl who was boss with a two ton truck. You're a real saint for stopping and calling 911."

I balled my right hand into a fist and took a step toward him. I caught a glimpse of a security guard's uniform out of the corner of my eye. I quickly stopped and dropped my hand. He was watching us as if he knew we were about to come to blows.

Instead of grabbing Danny and beating him to a pulp I rocked back on my heels and gave him my best smile. I spoke in a low, calm voice, and made sure he understood what was going to happen to him. "You have no clue what you're talking about, but I can tell you this, holy-roller. This isn't over by a long shot. I don't know how or when, but when you least expect it, I'll be there, ready to give you what you deserve."

I turned away from him, climbed in my truck, and slammed the door. I rolled down the window and threw in one parting shot. "I don't need your prayers, Jesus freak. Save them for yourself. Maybe your God can take away the stink of loser that always surrounds you like a fog."

I threw my head back and laughed as I backed out of the parking spot. I saluted him with my middle finger as I drove away.

CHAPTER THREE

I parked my truck in one of the open spaces by the football field. I rolled my window down and did a quick visual sweep of the field. Everything looked ready for the big game.

The white lines and hash marks gleamed in the fading afternoon light. The paint was fresh and unbroken. That wouldn't last long once all the guys got on the field. The scoreboard stood off to the side of the field, clean and freshly washed.

My stomach growled as the smell of chili and hot dogs filled my nose.

I love game night. There is nothing like it.

The only other people there that I could see were the cheerleaders. They stood on the sidelines, huddled around their coach.

I smiled, spending time with Ava was just what I needed to get my mind off of the crazy day and focus on the game.

I watched them for a minute. Ava stood off to the side by the water cooler. She was laughing at something her best friend Jenni said to her. Her ponytail bobbed up and down as she laughed.

Ava was the head cheerleader so obviously we needed to date. But was that all that kept us together? I remembered when we started dating. We laughed all the time. She was incredibly hot and the chemistry had been intense. We spent a lot of time making out and dreaming about the future.

Ava was the girl all the guys wanted to date and all the girls wanted to be. She was tall and thin, but not bony. Her hair looked like something out of a shampoo ad, pale blonde layers fell around her face and down past her shoulders. She had a way about her that when she looked at you it felt as if you were the only person in the room.

I thought hard as I tried to remember when we started drifting apart. Lately we only saw each other at school, football games, and the occasional party.

Fourth Down with Everything to Lose

When was the last time I'd seen her laugh like that at something I'd said? Irritated, I opened my door and slid out of the truck.

I started to walk across the field. Emma was wrong. My life was awesome. Everybody loved me, and I was going to prove it.

I missed a step and stumbled. "What the?" I muttered under my breath. Where on earth had that come from? I didn't have anything to prove to Emma. She was in a coma. I'd just seen her lying in a hospital bed. There was no way she had visited and taken me on a trip around the school to show me what everyone supposedly felt about me. It had to have been a dream. I'm the captain of the football team. What else is there to prove?

It didn't take the girls long to notice me. One of the younger girls, a cute redhead who giggles a lot started jumping up and down. "Hey gang, Ethan's here! Ethan's here!"

Another girl smiled at me and batted her eyes, "It's going to be an awesome game tonight Ethan. You guys are gonna crush the Hornets!"

I smiled at them and played into their flirting. "I don't know girls, the Hornets are pretty good…"

The redhead slapped my arm, "Stop it, Ethan Morgan. You know you guys are going to beat them. They can't hold a candle to you, Louis, and Tommy."

Feeling generous, I reached over, put my arm around her shoulder, and pulled her up against my side. "We couldn't do it without you beautiful ladies."

Her face turned red. I could feel her tremble. I looked over and noticed Ava watching us. I smiled and winked at her as she looked on. She didn't respond.

I gave the girl another squeeze, pulled away, and headed over to Ava. She stood still with her arms crossed over her middle. Her lips were pressed together and her eyes seemed almost wary as she watched me.

Something in her stance set me off. I could feel anger build as I walked the few short steps toward her. With a little more force than I intended, I reached for her, pulled her in close to my chest, and kissed her full on the lips. My hands reached around and locked her in my embrace. I could hear the other girls gasp.

Ava squirmed against me and managed to get her hands between us and put them on my chest. She pushed hard and tried to pull away. "Ethan, not in front of everyone."

My stomach dropped. She didn't want me to kiss her. My eyes locked on hers in a challenge, I called back over my shoulders to the other girls. "You girls don't mind if I kiss my best girl, do you?"

All I heard behind me was a bunch of breathless no's. I gave Ava a sarcastic smile and pulled her in again for another kiss. She didn't fight me this time, but it definitely wasn't the kind of kiss I was used to from her.

After I was done kissing her, I moved my lips to her ear and whispered, "You are *my* girl Ava. Don't forget that."

Her eyes widened in surprise. I reached over and gently twisted her ponytail in my hand and let her hair cascade through my fingers. I winked at her, "I'll see you after the game."

As I walked away she rubbed her bottom lip. Good. Maybe she'd remember she was my girl and start acting like it again.

....

By the second play of the game I had successfully pushed everything but the game out of my mind. I was able to zero in on my receivers, block the sound of the roaring crowd out of my mind, and concentrate on completing pass after pass.

The first quarter was over in a flash. We were up 20-3. We were marching down the field play after play. Tommy and Louis were catching every ball I threw in their direction. Our offensive line was mowing over the Hornet's defense. So far we had dominated every aspect of the game.

My heart pounded in my chest. This was the kind of game that could define my college career. Coach had mentioned the recruiters earlier in the week. I could feel their eyes on me, watching, reviewing, and judging my performance.

Toward the end of the second quarter, the Hornet's called a time out. I leaned over and put my hands on my knees. I made myself take some deep breaths and refocus on the game.

I wondered if dad had made it to the game. He usually had to work his second job on Friday nights. I could only remember him making a handful of games over the past three years. His excuse was work, but secretly I knew he was glad to have an excuse not to show. He wanted me to play and be successful, but I could tell he really didn't want to be around for it.

I stood up and let my eyes roam the stands. Maybe he'd made it.... I looked at all the parent's huddled together laughing and talking. I looked closely but my dad wasn't among the crowd. The next section of the stands was roped off for the nerd patrol, also known as the marching band. They were gathering their stuff getting ready to head down for half time.

Tommy interrupted my thoughts, "Hey Ethan, what now? What play you wanna run?"

I straightened up and looked over at the guys, "Let's run the long route."

"You sure about that Ethan?" Jesse asked.

I glared at him. "You got a better idea?"

He didn't reply. He dropped his eyes and shifted from his left foot to his right. I smiled. "That's what I thought. Just run your route. We've got this."

He held his hands up in surrender, "Whatever you say."

"Yeah, you got that right." I started to walk to the line when something caught my eye. An eerie mist swirled around the top of the stands. It was an odd mix of green and gold blended together. The mist seemed to surround one person. She sat off by herself with her chin propped in her hand. Her eyes were intense as she looked down at the field. Our eyes met. I missed a step and sucked in my breath. My heart slammed in my chest.

I looked around frantically and saw Tommy watching me. I pointed to the stands. "Do you see her Tommy? Emma's here. She's better. She's here!" I waived my hand toward the stands.

Tommy squinted his eyes and looked around, "What? Where is she? I don't see her... Ethan..."

"She's right there!" I exclaimed looking back at her as she sat enveloped in the mist. She raised her hand and gave me a little wave. "There. She just waived at me. Did you see it?"

He shook his head no, "Snap out of it Ethan, she's not there. We're gonna get a..."

The whistle blew. The referee motioned our side of the field. "Delay of game. Five yard penalty, still second down."

Coach threw his hands up and yelled from on the sideline. I couldn't hear him. All I could do was stare at Emma. Tommy was right, he couldn't see her. If she had actually been sitting in the bleachers, she'd be mobbed by a huge crowd. The fact that no one seemed to notice her or the mist confirmed my fear.

I pulled my eyes away from her and looked helplessly at Tommy. My legs felt stuck in quicksand. He grabbed my arm and pinched. "Snap out of it man. You're scaring everyone. What's wrong? Are you having a nervous breakdown? Dude your freaking me out."

He was freaked out? I jerked my arm free and shook off his hand. "I'm fine. Let's do this."

We moved into formation. I hunched over the center and called out the play, "32, 49, 32, hut, hut..." the ball was snapped, I ran back a few steps, caught the ball, pulled back my arm, and threw it high and long.

It looked good as it sailed up and through the air. Tommy leaped in the air and reached out with his hands but instead of coming down with the ball he collided with a corner back.

The ball bounced out of Tommy's hands and landed perfectly in the corner backs outstretched hands. He pulled the ball to his chest, regained his footing, and took off for the end zone. He made it past our entire offensive line and ran straight for me. I threw myself at him and caught his ankle. He shook me off and ran the rest of the way down the field to score a touchdown.

The buzzer sounded signaling the end of the first half.

As I jogged toward the locker room, my eyes flew back to where I'd seen Emma sitting up in the stands. The weird mist I'd seen earlier was gone. There was no sign of her anywhere.

．．．．．．．

When the game finally ended, I packed up my stuff and drove over to Grady's house. Grady lives on a huge farm outside town. A lot of the team and their girls end up there on Friday nights to celebrate our wins or lick our wounds after a tough loss. His parents always want us to hang out. His mom says that at least that way she knows where we are and what we're doing.

As I drove, I beat myself up over the game. Somehow, we'd managed to win the game. It wasn't pretty but we held off the Hornets to get the win. No thanks to my delusions.

After I'd seen Emma I struggled to get my head back in the game. I pounded my hands against the steering wheel in frustration. It had taken me until the fourth quarter to pull myself together, but even that had more to do with Coach screaming at me and threatening to pull me from the game than my desire to play. I've been the quarterback since my sophomore year, no way was I getting benched as a senior.

I pulled into Grady's driveway and drove back the tree lined lane to the house. I parked my truck and watched as people came and went from the house. Light spilled out of the windows onto the ground. The porch was full of kids hanging out. I could hear the faint beat of the music blaring from inside. Grady's parents had gone on some kind of marriage retreat for the weekend, so this promised to be a different party than we normally had every week. They'd given him specific instructions not to have a big party, just a few friends. From what I could see, this small party already had about fifty people here. So much for small.

My thoughts shifted to Ava. I was anxious to see her and figure out what was going on. She's been my girlfriend for a long time. I couldn't imagine her with another guy. I am the captain of the football team. She is the head cheerleader. We are a power couple at school.

I got out of the truck and walked up the sidewalk and into the house. The music became considerably louder when I opened the front door and stepped inside.

I shoved my way through the crowd ignoring the yelps as I stepped on toes. Kids were perched on every available surface. I ignored the greetings called out to me as I pushed my way through the stream of people standing in my way. I wasn't in the mood to be social. I wanted answers.

I didn't get why I kept seeing Emma. I was starting to believe that maybe I was really seeing her, that it wasn't a dream or hallucination. This time I was awake in the middle of a football field when I saw her.

I could argue that it was just someone who looked like her, or maybe the setting sun reflecting off the bleachers. Maybe I needed glasses.

If what I'd seen was real, then the dreams, or whatever they were, might be real too. I don't understand how it's possible, but that didn't make it any less real. It opened a whole boatload of questions in my mind.

I walked into the kitchen and caught Jesse and Ava laughing. His head was bent down close to hers. She wasn't pushing him away. When they saw me, they jumped apart and tried to act like nothing was going on. If Emma's visits were real, then there was definitely something going on between these two. Anger washed over me. Ava was my girlfriend. She was supposed to be loyal to me.

I casually walked over and slapped Jesse really hard on the back. "Hey guys, what's up?"

I hit Jesse so hard, it knocked some wind out of him. He sucked in air and glared at me, "What was that for?"

"Sorry, didn't know you were such a wuss." I looked at Ava. I gave her a big smile, "Hey babe, where'd you go after the game?" I put my arm around her and pulled her close.

"I figured you'd need some time alone so I rode over with the girls. I knew you'd be here eventually." She reached up and touched my cheek. "You okay?"

I looked into her big blue eyes and part of me wanted to tell her everything. I suddenly just wanted to put my head in her lap and let it all out. The accident, the visits from Emma, all of it.

We stared at each other for several seconds. Her eyes seemed to be asking me to confide in her. I decided why not and opened my mouth to say something, but I didn't get the chance to say anything. Louis strutted in the room already talking, "Dude what happened to you out there? We thought you were having a seizure!"

Just that fast the moment was gone. I saw the disappointment in Ava's eyes. She looked away and took a step back away from my arms.

Irritated, I turned to face Louis. I shrugged my shoulders and tried to look unconcerned. "Migraine. I don't know why, but when we were in the huddle, a nasty migraine hit. I'm fine now."

Louis leaned against the counter, "A migraine? You don't get headaches. I can't even remember the last time you had a cold. Maybe you should go to the doctor."

"I don't need a doctor." I snapped. "What I need is a wide receiver who can catch the ball and not make excuses." I reached over and grabbed Ava's arm. "Come on Ava, let's get out of here."

I practically drug her back through the living room and out the front door. I was out of breath by the time we made it my truck. When I stopped, she yanked her arm free of my grasp and glared at me. "What are you doing, Ethan?'

I gave her a smile. "I don't know Ava. Maybe I just want to get out of here. Be alone with my girlfriend. Is that a crime?"

She shook her head. "I don't think that's a good idea."

"Why the hell not? When was the last time we did anything just the two of us? We spend so much time with those half-wits that I think we've forgotten how to be a couple. When was the last time we…"

"Ethan…." She interrupted me. "Not here." She put her hand up to stop me as I moved toward her. Angry, I grabbed her wrist and yanked her up against me.

"What's the problem Ava? Why don't you want to be alone with me anymore? Don't you want to make me happy? You're my girlfriend. You're supposed to want to spend time with me." I let go of her wrist and grabbed both her arms. I pulled her in for a kiss. It wasn't a nice kiss. I was angry and I needed to know she still cared about me, not some other guy. I pushed her against the truck and kept kissing her, my hands started to roam over her arms and across her stomach.

I would've kept going, but I stopped mid kiss when I tasted a tear. I jerked back and stared at her. Tears streaked down her cheeks. I felt like someone poured ice cold water over my head. Who was I? I didn't force myself on girls. I cupped her chin in my hand and forced her to look up at me. I could see fear in her eyes. It made my stomach churn. "Why are you crying Ava?" I whispered.

"You're scaring me." She whispered back. She broke eye contact and looked somewhere over my shoulder as tears continued to fall.

I let go of her chin and pulled her against my chest. "You don't have to be scared of me." I rested my chin on top of her head and sighed. "What's happening to us? You didn't used to be scared of me. What happened?"

"I don't know. You're so angry all the time. And…"

I pulled back to look down at her face, "And what?"

She looked away briefly, sighed and looked back at me. Sadness filled her eyes. "Ethan, you've changed. You're mean. Really mean. It's not funny anymore. You pick a fight with everyone. You act like we all belong to you."

"Seriously?" I snapped pushing her away from me. "That's what you think of me?"

She didn't respond. I was at a loss for words. I glared at her and tried to find something to say, but I couldn't. The scene in the gym kept looping through my head.

After several uncomfortable seconds, I pointed my finger at her. "Funny how you say that, now that you've reaped the rewards of being a star quarterback's girlfriend. I remember when we met, you thought I was the best thing ever. You couldn't get enough of me while you were climbing to the top of the pyramid. You laughed at my jokes and pranks. In fact, if memory serves, you asked me to do some of those very pranks." I threw my hands up in the air, "Now all of a sudden I'm scary?"

"Ethan..."

"You know what? I don't have time for this crap. If you want Jesse, you can have him. I'm done, but don't you dare come crawling to me when you're suddenly nothing again. Because that's what you are without me. NOTHING!" I shoved her away from my truck, walked around to the driver's side, got in, and peeled out of the driveway.

....

Thankfully the house was dark and quiet when I got home. I was in no mood to update my dad on the game and hear what he had to say about my interception. To say he would be disappointed was an understatement. Plus I was still pissed over what Ava had said to me.

I walked through the kitchen and started down the hall toward the stairs. I noticed the light from the television flashing shades of blue and gray on the wall. Quietly, I made my way down the hall and peeked into the den. Dad was fast asleep in his recliner. His head was tipped back and the sound of snoring filled the room. I glanced at the television. One of those stupid crime shows where you can guess the killer in the first ten minutes was playing.

My eyes drifted back to my dad. He was holding something square in his hand. I took a step forward to see what it was he was holding. My breath caught in my throat. He was holding the last picture we had of mom. My chest tightened uncomfortably as I looked down at it.

My mom knelt on the ground beside me. She had a huge smile on her face. I did too. I was grinning from ear to ear as I held a squirming baby goat in my hands.

I hadn't thought about that day in a long time. I had begged and begged for days to go to the small county fair our town hosted every year. My dad finally said yes so we packed up the car and took off for the fair. We spent the day looking at animals, watching tractor pulls, and eating cotton candy.

While we were sitting on a bench, a baby goat had gotten away from its handler and was running down the aisle straight toward us. I managed to catch him by the collar as he darted past. We walked him back to his worried owner. Mom and dad were so proud of me as I led it back to its pen.

I blinked several times to fight tears that threatened to fall. That was the last good picture we had of mom. Two weeks later she had been diagnosed with an aggressive brain tumor and three months later, she died. Just like that, the sweetest and kindest person I'd ever known had been ripped away from us.

Dad and I spent that entire summer and early fall taking her to doctors, hoping for a miracle all the while watching her go from the woman we knew and loved to someone we didn't recognize.

Brain tumors aren't remotely like the way they are portrayed on television. The person doesn't just lose weight, dole out sad goodbyes, and die quietly in their sleep. They lose their minds, literally. At the end my mom couldn't feed herself, she had no control over what she said, and she screamed in pain.

I ran my hand over her face. Gently, I put the picture on my dad's arm rest. I turned and walked out of the room as fast as my feet would carry me. I still missed her so much. It had been years since I'd allowed myself to remember the end. What it had been like to watch her suffer and finally understand she was going to die. I'd worked hard to stuff those feelings down. Remembering was just to freaking painful.

I jogged up the stairs to my room and collapsed on the end of the bed. I put my head in my hands. Tears streamed down my cheeks. My body heaved from sobs that seemed to come up from the depths of my stomach. The pain was so intense it was as if she had just died. Ten years of denying what I'd felt bubbled up and out of me.

A long time passed. When I couldn't cry anymore I stood to my feet and shuffled over to the window. I leaned against the window frame and looked out over the backyard.

My thoughts drifted back over the last few days. Maybe Ava was right, maybe I was too mean. After all, if I hadn't wanted to torment Emma, she'd be out with her friends right now. Instead, because of my bullying, she was fighting for her life in a hospital bed.

The past few days had started to unravel the threads of the perfect life I'd built for myself. Could it be that people actually feared me instead of truly liking me? Was I the monster Ava and Emma thought I was? When had I become so angry? When did my relationships become based on fear instead of friendship? Was Emma right? Did I even have any true friends?

CHAPTER FOUR

The ball spiraled down the length of the football field toward the uprights. Cheers from the bleachers carried on the air as the excitement of the play built. Tommy, my wide receiver of choice, stretched his arms up, and leaped into the air. His fingers wrapped around the ball. He tucked it to his chest and surged forward as soon as his feet connected with the ground. He pushed forward dodging the defense as they dove first for his waist, then his feet, and finally they were left scrambling to tackle whatever part of his body they could hit.

As Tommy's foot stretched out to cross the goal line, a loud clap sounded, and I jerked awake. I sat straight up in bed. Thunder boomed and rolled across the sky. I glanced over at the window as several streaks of lightening flashed and lit up my otherwise dark room. The flashes of light were followed quickly by another boom so strong that it rattled the window.

I fell back against my pillows and closed my eyes. My shoulders relaxed against the pillow. I told myself to breathe and go back to sleep. It was just a storm. No big deal.

Five minutes later I let out a heavy sigh and opened my eyes again. I knew sleep wasn't coming anytime soon. I propped myself up on my elbow to see what time it was and choked back a scream. Emma was standing by the alarm clock.

"Oh my God, will you stop doing that?" I snapped.

She threw her head back and laughed. "Priceless."

I rolled my eyes. "I'm glad you find this amusing. What are you doing here anyway?" I strained to see the alarm clock, it read 4:22am. "I have to be up for work in 2 hours." I flopped back and covered my eyes with my hands. "Can't this wait? I have a full day ahead of me. I just want to sleep."

"No can do. It's now or never."

"I pick never. Go away."

I heard her move around the bed. I opened my left eye just enough to peek out at her. She was standing by the bed with her arms crossed in front of her chest. She didn't look amused. I sighed and sat up.

"Better." She stated smiling.

"So it wasn't enough that you ruined my game tonight? You have to come bother me while I'm trying to sleep?"

"It was a pretty hard game to watch. You seemed... kind of... flustered." She agreed.

"Is it any wonder? I'm having the game of the year. Hitting all my marks when out of the blue, I look up in the stands and see a weird light and there you are perched in the stands. Then, stupid me, I ask Tommy if he can see you too."

"You didn't! Did you?"

"Uh, yeah, I did. When he looked at me like I was two doughnuts shy of a dozen, I tried to blame a headache. My entire team thinks I'm either crazy or having seizures."

Emma's laugh surprised me. She covered her mouth with her hand. "Sorry." She tried to apologize as she continued to laugh.

I rolled my eyes. "Why were you there anyway?"

She shrugged. "I was bored. Being in a coma isn't all that exciting."

I snorted in disbelief. "If you're bored, why don't you just wake up and get better? Then you won't be bored anymore and you can leave me alone."

Her eyes moved away from my face and her smile faded away. "I'm not sure I'll get better."

After a lengthy pause, she looked back at me and smiled again. "What I do know, is that I have a week to make you see the error of your ways. God has a purpose for you. Whether you like it or not, he has his eye on you."

"That's crazy. God doesn't even exist. I don't need you to save me."

"Apparently you do. Now come on, we've got places to go, people to see."

"I'd rather not."

"Well, I'd rather be planning my date for the homecoming dance. We don't always get what we want."

I swung my legs over the side of the bed and glared at her. She just stared back at me. Finally I broke eye contact. "Whatever, let's just get this over with."

Stomping over to my closet, I slipped my feet into a pair of blue sneakers. I turned back to face her and suddenly found myself standing in another room. Dark green shag carpet covered the floor. A plaid couch was pushed against the wall. We were standing in the basement of Emma's house right after they had moved in. We played in this basement every Saturday night for over a year until her dad couldn't take the shag carpet anymore. He, along with my dad, and a couple of other friends, ripped the whole thing apart and updated it with new carpet, a pool table and leather furniture. I had a lot of memories of times spent playing here.

Me, Emma, and a bunch of kids from church would play down here for hours while our parents had bible studies and prayer meetings. I looked over at the corner where we always built forts to fend off the alien dinosaurs or pirates. Then I glanced at the doorway of the laundry room and shook my head as I remembered all the haunted houses we'd created in there. The musty smell, dark corners, and shelves blended together to make an awesomely creepy atmosphere.

A scream burst through the room causing me to jump. I watched as a younger version of myself ran out of the laundry room screaming and laughing. A younger Emma ran after me yelling, "I'll get you my pretty and your little dog too." A tall, black pointed hat was perched precariously on her head and she clutched a broom that was taller than she was. Her dark brown eyes sparkled in glee as she chased the younger me around cackling and waving her arms.

I watched the other me jump on the old overstuffed couch and squeal as Emma came charging after him.

"I'm safe. I'm safe, I'm on base!"

She stopped short of the couch, frowning, "No fair Ethan, you have to give me a chance to catch you."

"It's not my fault I'm faster than you are."

"That's not true! I had to stay in character and keep my hat on."

"Oh well, then I win, I made it out of the dark forest before you could catch me."

Emma leaned on the broom, "So what now? Do you want to play dragon and princess?"

"No cause you never want to be the princess."

"Princesses are stupid. I want to be strong. I don't need a prince to rescue me."

I chuckled as our exchange played out in front of me. I'd forgotten how much fun we'd had playing together. Emma's imagination always had us chasing dragons, building castles, or roping dinosaurs. She was always willing to get dirty and make up all sorts of games.

I looked over at her. She was watching the younger versions of us with an intent expression on her face.

"We were something weren't we?" I whispered.

She nodded her head and smiled a smile I hadn't seen in a very long time. Her tone was wistful as she answered me. " I used to love when you and your parents would come over."

I nodded my head. "We had a lot of fun."

"We sure did."

I pushed away the sad feeling that was threatening to overcome me and said, "But as usual you wouldn't be the princess. You always wanted to do the saving." I sighed, "Some things never change."

She chuckled, "I guess not."

....

Emma crossed the distance between us and touched my arm. Suddenly I found myself standing in a hospital. The hair on my arms stood up, it wasn't just any hospital. It was Oakdale Medical Center. I fought the urge to run as the familiar smell of antiseptic crept up my nose and filled my mouth. I've spent years trying to forget that awful blend of cleaner, sickness, and fear. The smell crept up my nose and through my entire body.

Overcome by the smell, I coughed into my hand until I thought I was going to throw up. Bending at the knees, I put my hands on my legs and tried to drag some air in through my mouth. Anything to avoid that stench.

When I collected myself, I snapped. "What are we doing here?"

"I think you know." Emma stated calmly. My eyes flew to her face. She was staring at the door across the hall from us.

My eyes darted back and forth from her to the door. I shook my head violently, "Un-huh. No way. I know where we are and I'm not doing this." I pointed my finger at her. "You have no right to make me do this."

Before Emma could respond, a deep moan drifted out of the room. My entire body convulsed. I remembered that hideous sound all too well. My throat constricted. I threw a desperate look at Emma. My eyes begged hers, "Seriously…" I choked out, " I can't do… this …again."

A flash of orange caught my eye. A small boy about eight years old ran out of the room. He ran to the window at the end of the hallway and planted his small hands against the glass. His fingers bent as if he were trying to dig his way through to get outside. He balled his hands into fists and pounded the glass. Suddenly as fast as he'd started pummeling the window he became limp and let his body slide down the wall until he was sitting on the floor.

I watched the boy as pain stabbed through my chest. The little boy was me. I remembered the Bengal's sweatshirt all too well. I had begged and begged for a Carson Palmer Sweatshirt until finally my mom had surprised me with it one night after dinner. My dad had rolled his eyes and exclaimed that she was spoiling me. She'd just laughed and said that's what mom's do. They spoil their sons.

I crossed the hallway and knelt down beside him. I looked up at Emma. "He can't see me?"

"No." She shook her head. Tears glistened in her eyes.

I looked at the door of the hospital room. I could make out the shadow of my dad as he sat vigil by my mom's bed. I knew the hard way that he wouldn't come get me. In fact he never came looking for me.

I got to my feet and turned toward Emma. Anger surged through me. "This is crap. How in the world does my mom's death have anything to do with me? So what if I pick on some dorky kids?" I crossed my arms and glared at her.

"Ethan. You need to make peace with what happened. It's holding you prisoner and you don't even know it."

I rolled my eyes and started to make a snide remark when a young nurse came striding around the corner. She stopped cold at the sight of the younger me huddled under the window. She was a tall woman with dark hair and eyes. Her skin was the color of caramel. The whiteness of her scrubs stood out in stark contrast to her skin. She held a pile of charts in her hands. A loose curl of hair fell across her forehead, giving her otherwise impeccable bun a less severe look. Her eyes flashed with sadness and concern when she saw the younger version of me huddled under the window. She set the pile of charts on the window sill and knelt down.

"Hey there young man, are you okay?"

The younger me shook his head no and hiccupped. She eased herself down to the floor beside him and put her arm around him. He flinched and drew away. She tried again and he sagged against her side. She pulled him close and let him cry against her spotless scrubs.

She held him until he was cried out, all the while rubbing his arm and murmuring, "There, there, let it out honey. I'm not going anywhere."

When he was cried out, he pulled back and glared at her. "I don't need you to hug me, you know."

I heard Emma sigh behind me.

The nurse smiled and shrugged. "I know that honey. I needed you. I'm having a rough day. I thought a hug would help."

He perked up and wiped his eyes. "Did it?"

"Always does. I can't remember the last time a good hug didn't make things just a little better."

He looked down at his hands. "My mom's here. She's dying."

"I'm sorry to hear that." She didn't fuss, she just stated the obvious.

"Thanks." He sniffed loudly and wiped his nose on his sleeve.

She pulled out some tissues and handed them to him. "Here you go, just in case."

"Ok." He nodded clutching them in his fist.

She stood up and held her hand out. "Think you might want to go back in to see your mom?"

He got to his feet and dusted off his pants. Then he looked at the door across the hallway. I felt the despair and terror all over again. He took a deep breath and sighed, "I guess."

The nurse leaned down until their faces were inches apart. She gave him a small smile. "I know this is the hardest thing you've ever had to do, but someday, probably not for many years, but someday honey, you will be glad you did. If it gets to be too much, go to the nurse's station and ask for Agnes. I will be more than glad to sit with you, talk, listen, whatever you need. You got that?"

He nodded his head yes and choked back more tears. Agnes straightened up, grabbed her charts, and started off down the hall. She called back over her shoulder, "Remember, ask for Agnes if you need anything at all."

He nodded and watched her walk away.

I followed the younger version of myself to the door of my mom's room. We both paused in the doorway to try and work up the courage to go inside. I glanced over at Emma. She gave me a smile and nodded her head.

When I stepped into the room, the last ten years melted away and inside I felt as young and vulnerable as the boy version of myself standing beside me.

My eyes swept the room. I could see my dad. He sat in a small straight backed chair by her bed. His shoulders were hunched as he leaned forward clasping her right hand. The only light in the room came in from the hallway. The blinds were closed tight. The room was cloaked in dark shadows.

The room had an air of stillness that was eerie. Even the machines with their beeps and chirps seemed to understand it was time to whisper and be still.

My eyes finally came to rest on the hospital bed. I sucked in a deep breath. Huddled under several blankets was what was left of my mom. Her body was swallowed up in the covers. She had the appearance of a really old woman, but she was only in her late twenties. Her once beautiful blonde hair was thin and stringy. She'd lost most of it to various treatments and procedures. Even more had fallen out when she stopped eating.

As the younger version of me worked up the courage to approach the bed, I did too. Moving forward those few steps was like trying to walk through a newly poured sidewalk. My legs felt heavy as if I were wearing concrete boots.

We stopped side by side facing my mom. My dad didn't even look up. He sat in his chair oblivious to the fact that someone else was in the room. Anger washed over me. Why didn't he reach out and pull me close? Tell me it was going to be okay? Instead he just stared at mom like he was completely lost.

My mom's eyes flickered open. She gave the younger me a weak smile. The effort made her wince in pain. "Ethan."

She recognized me, at the end that hadn't always been the case. I watched him step closer to her and reach out to touch her briefly on the side with his small hand.

"Hey mom." He choked out.

"Hey honey. You look awfully… handsome…today."

"Don't talk mom, save your strength." The younger me pleaded with her.

Her lips twitched in a small smile, "I don't think it… matters now… Ethan."

Tears coursed down both of our cheeks. She pulled her hand free from dad and motioned me closer. The younger me leaned in. She sighed a big sigh, "Ethan honey, I love you… so much."

"I love you too Mom." I whispered alongside the younger version of myself. Tears slid down my face. I reached out and tried to touch her. My hand just moved through her as if she were a hologram.

"I know you do baby. Will…. you do something… for me?"

The younger me nodded his head vigorously, "Anything Mom."

"Your such a… good boy….", she smiled wistfully. "Please… take care… of your…dad. He needs…" her last word never came. The monitor went haywire, the beeping grew exponentially louder and then suddenly started making one long continuous beep.

My dad flew up out of his chair and ran out into the hallway screaming, "We need help in here. Please hurry!"

The room filled instantly with hospital staff and harsh white lights. My dad followed them into the room waving his hands, "Please help her, oh God, please help her."

The younger me was shoved back out of the way against the wall. Doctors and nurses clamored with equipment while my dad paced in the back of the room yelling, "Do something! Don't let her die…"

Watching the scene play out again was too much. Pain erupted in my chest and brought me to my knees. I went to the floor sobbing. The pain of watching what I'd gone through again was too much to bear. I wanted to help so badly. Reach out to the younger me and hug him tight. Instead all I could do was watch as he backed out of the room with his eyes opened in absolute terror.

My stomach heaved from the force of the sobs that were tearing through my body. When I couldn't take the pain anymore, the room faded away and I suddenly found myself surrounded by battered playground equipment.

Kneeling on the asphalt, it took me several minutes to pull myself together. When the pain started to subside, I stopped crying, and slowly stood to my feet. Every muscle and joint in my body throbbed with pain and stiffness. I wrapped my arms across my chest and rubbed my hands up and down them to help ease the pain.

I tried to figure out where I was. I looked around at all the playground equipment. The chipped paint on the teeter-totter brought back memories. This was my old elementary playground. The old monkey bars, slides, and swings were lined up on the concrete, ready to be used. I walked over and tried to touch the slide. My hand went through it. I sighed. Would this nightmare ever end?

I jumped as a loud bell clanged against the side of the school. Seconds later kids came flying through the side doors. In no time flat, every piece of equipment was being used, kids were laughing, and the sound of recess filled the air.

I looked around, but didn't see Emma. I turned back to watch the kids play and watched a young boy in blue pants and a checkered shirt cross the monkey bars, only he didn't make it all the way. He fell onto the concrete below. When he stood up, his knee was bloody. He turned his head and I gasped. It was me!

Once again I was watching a younger version of myself. I noticed as I watched him walk across the playground there was something different about him now. His face was hard and his eyes didn't sparkle. This wasn't the same kid that had let Emma chase him through the basement with a broom. His stride was stiff, his fists clenched at his side.

A small girl with a long ponytail in a flower print dress ran up to him. "Ethan, are you okay? You're bleeding!"

He stopped and glared at the girl, "I'm fine. Leave me alone."

I walked around them and as I suspected the girl was Emma. She jerked back from his harsh words. "I was just worried."

"Well, don't be," he snapped. He started toward the teacher again. Emma followed him.

She waited until the teacher put a Band-Aid on his knee and he walked back toward the swings. She approached him again. "Hey Ethan, are you coming to Sunday school this week?"

"Hardly." He snorted. "Why would I want to go to Sunday school? It's for losers."

Emma stepped in front of him and crossed her arms, "Ethan, are you mad at me?"

He stopped and put his hands on his hips. "No, I'm not mad at you. I hate you."

Her face paled. "Why? What did I do?" She grabbed his arm, "You're my best friend."

He shoved her. She fell backward and landed on her butt on the concrete. "No, I'm not. I can't be your friend anymore!"

"Why not?" She cried.

"Because you're a loser. Anyone who believes in God is a total loser!!!" He screamed at her before turning and running off across the playground.

I sighed. I had totally forgotten that day. I knew Emma and I had words and we stopped being friends. I didn't remember it was so close to my mom's death. The younger version of Emma stood up, brushed off her pants and wiped away tears that were running down her cheeks, and made her way slowly back to the door as the bell rang to end recess.

I looked to find Emma standing beside the merry-go-round. Sadness emanated from her eyes as she watched the younger version of herself. I fought the urge to say something. A feeling of unease washed over me. I'd hurt her, over and over, I had hurt her. Why? Anger bubbled up inside me, I didn't like the way she was making me feel.

"Are we done yet? This is so lame. I don't know how you expected me to react. We were kids. So we didn't stay best friends. Big deal. Lots of kids don't stay friends."

Emma looked at me, her eyes filled with anger. "Seriously Ethan? I never thought you were stupid. Maybe I was wrong." She walked over and sat on the merry-go-round.

"Stupid? I'm definitely not stupid. Why don't you just say what you have to say instead of showing me all this crap." I swung my arms wide to make my point. "I don't understand why any of this is necessary."

"Fine, you want honest, how's this for honest? You let your mom's death pull you away from everyone who cared about you, including God. You made yourself into this tough, no nonsense guy who doesn't know how to be a friend to anyone. And, you let your dad's weaknesses take over your life until you didn't have a place for God."

"So what! Maybe I don't need God or even want Him in my life. Why do you care so much?"

"Because if you don't change, bad things are going to happen, and I can't stand that thought." Her eyes pleaded with mine. "You were my best friend for a long time. We share a lot of fun childhood memories. And, yes, some bad ones too, but I care about you. Whether you care about me or not, I will always care about what happens to you."

I threw my arms up in the air, "This is crazy. Emma, I'm sorry I treated you so lousy. I was a jerk. I totally admit that. I will try to do better, but as far as God is concerned, I don't believe in Jesus, or hell. In fact I don't believe in any of it."

Emma's right eyebrow arched as she crossed her arms. She stared at me until I started to fidget. When she spoke her tone was laced with sarcasm. "I guess we'll see about that."

CHAPTER FIVE

"Not yet…" I groaned as music blared from my alarm clock. Without opening my eyes, I slapped my hand on the nightstand until I found the snooze button. Thankfully the music stopped as fast as it started. I rolled over onto my back and stared at the ceiling.

My head pounded and my eyes felt swollen and scratchy. I rubbed them and wondered when I was going to get a decent night's sleep. The events of the night before played through my mind: the visit from Emma, reliving some of our past, and watching my mom die again.

I sat up and sighed. Everything was getting way too complicated. I needed to push all that mushy crap out of my mind. It had never done me any good to dwell on the sad stuff. No one cared and no one wanted to deal with my crappy past. I threw the covers off and climbed out of bed.

I took a shower and dressed quickly. I hoped that maybe my dad would already be gone. He usually picked up an extra shift or two over the weekend so I was hopeful that I might get lucky and miss him.

I jogged down the stairs and into the kitchen and skidded to a stop in the doorway. No such luck. There he sat at the table with a cup of coffee and the newspaper in front of him. I walked to the refrigerator and opened it to find the milk.

I heard him sigh. My shoulders tensed. I knew what was coming.

"Well you sure screwed that up last night." He rattled the newspaper. "Your interception made the paper. Want me to read you the headline?"

I didn't answer, I opened the cabinet and grabbed a glass. I knew he didn't want to hear what I had to say so I kept my mouth shut and leaned against the counter.

"Shining Light a Little Dimmer After Car Accident. Is the Magic Gone?" He slammed the newspaper on the table. I jumped.

"What in the hell happened to you last night?"

"I don't know Dad. I guess I didn't feel so great."

"Excuse me?" He raised his eyebrow and mocked me, "You weren't feeling well? When has that ever mattered? Athletes don't get the luxury of being sick. You have to play through the pain. Push past the distractions."

I chanced a glance at him. "I'm sorry. I've been a little bit preoccupied by what happened the other night."

He flopped back in his chair and crossed his arms. "What is there to be preoccupied about? That girl will either get better or she won't. You didn't do anything wrong it was an accident."

A flare of anger shot through me. "That girl has a name." I snapped. "It's Emma Montgomery. You know, Mike and Carol Montgomery's daughter, Emma? She's hurt really bad. I stopped in to see her yesterday, it doesn't look good…"

"You did what?" He yelled, standing up. "You went to the hospital to see her?" When I nodded he threw his hands up in the air. "I give up. When are you going to do what I tell you to do?"

"Maybe it showed I'm not some unfeeling monster. Despite what you want, I'm not just a machine that goes to school, plays football, and sits quietly in his room. Dad, I hit her. It doesn't matter how it happened. I hit her and she's in a coma in the hospital and she might even die. I would think that should make me feel bad and I should want to see if she's okay. What do you want me to do? Act like it never happened?"

He shook his finger at me. "Yes! That's exactly what I want you to do. You can't let this bring all of your dreams to a crashing halt. You have to buck up and get over it. You have three games left this season. You need to make every one of them count. You have to be the best player on the field every time you go out and play. This is where it counts. Get your head back in the game before it's too late."

I slammed my glass down in the sink and walked to the back door. "You know what Dad? Thanks for asking if I'm okay. Thanks for giving a crap that I wasn't seriously hurt the other night. Oh, and, thanks for making sure I'm not traumatized from what happened. Don't worry about your only son. No need to get emotionally involved. I'm sure I'll just get over it, like I have all the other stressful moments in my life. You can keep drinking beer and hiding in your den."

I opened the back door and shouted back over my shoulder, "You know something really sad? I wish I had been the one diagnosed with a brain tumor. At least then I'd be the one who died and you'd still have mom. That's how you've always wanted it anyway."

I didn't stick around to hear his response. I'd had enough. I had to be at the feed store at 9:00am for my shift. Anywhere was better than home so I got in my truck and took off. It seemed like I was doing that a lot lately.

....

"Hey, superstar, what happened last night?"

I forced a smile as I heaved a fifty pound bag of dog food into the back of Mr. Evans truck. He leaned against the side of his truck and chewed on a broken straw.

"I don't know, Mr. Evans. Guess it was just a rough night. We still won the game."

"That you did, son. That you did, but it seems to me, you were a bit distracted. Everything okay?"

I shrugged. "Yeah, everything's fine. I guess the accident the other night threw me off my game."

Mr. Evans nodded his head and pointed the straw at me, "You did good calling 911 the other night. The Montgomery's are good people. I remember little Emma when she was a baby. My Sarah babysat her on Tuesdays so her mama could go to one of them weight loss meetings. Emma always followed me around asking questions. Are you two friends?"

"Nah." I replied. "We used to be, but not so much anymore."

Mr. Evans moved to the driver's side door of his truck and opened the door. "That's a shame, Ethan. She's a good kid."

"Yes, sir."

He slid behind the wheel and poked his head out the window. "Maybe when she gets better, you can change that." He winked at me, put his truck in drive, and pulled away.

I sagged against a stack of hay bales and watched him drive off.

Exhaustion swept through me. I typically love my job at the Feed Mill. I get to talk to a lot of people. Usually the topic of conversation is my latest record breaking game or what's going on in town. Not today. All everyone wanted to talk about was last night's game and the accident. As I watched Mr. Evans drive away, I was ready to punch the next person who gave me a look of pity, or asked why my game had been so off the night before. Seriously, didn't they have anything better to talk about?

It was finally 3:00p.m. so I untied my apron and made my way to the front of the store. Bill, the manager waived me over to the counter.

"What's up, Bill?"

"Hey, Ethan, I just got some unsettling news. My cousin Sally, the one who works at the hospital, said she heard Emma has taken a turn for the worse. The doctors think she might have pneumonia."

He came out from behind the counter and put his arm around my shoulders and squeezed. "I thought you might want to know. You hang in there. She's a tough girl. She'll be alright."

It took all the effort I had to nod and thank him. I felt like the bottom just fell out from under me. This was bad. She was still getting worse. Suddenly I couldn't get enough air. I disengaged from him as quickly as I could and practically ran out of the store. I got in my truck and started driving. I had no idea where I was going. My head was spinning and I felt sick to my stomach.

I drove around for a long time. I kept making turns and twisting through town. I didn't want to go home. I didn't want to deal with my dad and I couldn't go to the football field. Louis, Grady, and the guys wouldn't be any help. I didn't know where to go or who to turn to.

I turned onto Maple Street and slowed to a crawl. Up ahead on the right was a big old church. It stood tall and proud, with a white steeple, stained glass windows, and ornate trim. I slowed to a stop and stared at it through my window.

I looked at the big old building and tried to find some comfort. This was the church my parents had gotten married in.

I'd gone to Sunday school and vacation bible school here. I had a lot of early memories of this place. Even though the building itself hadn't changed much, I felt like a stranger as I sat and stared at it.

I'm not sure why, but I opened the door of the truck, got out, and walked up the steps. I ran my hand along the banister. This building had housed a lot of different churches. I think it started out as a Lutheran church but over the years it had changed hands and even sat empty for a while. Now it's called the Oakdale Community Church.

I reached out and tried the door. I figured it would be locked. It wasn't; it opened right up. The old familiar smells of lemon pledge, musty books, and faded perfume washed over me. It brought back so many memories.

I stopped in the back of the sanctuary as one memory in particular came rushing back to me. I'd kissed my first girl here when I was six. It had been Emma. We'd just finished up practice for the Christmas play. We were still in our costumes waiting for our parents to arrive. I'd pulled her pigtail and told her that Mary wouldn't have worn pigtails with red rubber bands. She got mad, punched my arm, and started to chase me. We ran around the pews until finally, to exhausted to run anymore, we collapsed on the last pew in the back.

Emma promptly informed me she would wear whatever color rubber bands she wanted to because Jesus loved her. I'd rolled my eyes and said, "Whatever". The next thing I knew, she reached over and planted a kiss on my lips and then jumped up and took off. We never said anything about it to each other ever again.

I glanced at the pew where the kiss had taken place. Everything looked the same. The way the wood gleamed in the fading light. The colors from the stain glass window dancing around the sanctuary. It was still a beautiful church. I felt the weight of all the memories I'd made here press down on me. My heart felt heavier than it had in a long time.

I walked about half down the aisle and slid into one of the pews. I hadn't been in a church since my mom died. I remember clearly the day I vowed I would never step foot inside one again. I looked at the pictures around the room. Jesus was everywhere. I felt anger build inside me. Who was He? Why didn't He save my mom? Did He exist? Why was He letting Emma suffer? If He was so awesome, why didn't He heal her? Anger churned around inside of me like a tornado.

Absorbed in my thoughts, I didn't hear the man approach until he said my name.

"Ethan Morgan?"

My head snapped up to see who was talking to me. I couldn't believe it. It was Jason Corbett. He was only the best quarterback Oakdale had ever seen, until me that is. I've smashed almost every record he had at our school. He was a legend. He played in the NFL for about five years. What in the world was he doing back in Oakdale?

He grinned at me and held out his hand. "It's great to finally meet you in person, Ethan. I've heard a lot about how you're demolishing all of my football records."

I shook his hand and smiled back at him. "I'm doing what I can."

He threw back his head and laughed. "Mind if I join you for a minute?"

I shook my head, "Not at all."

"What brings you here today?" He asked sitting down on the pew in front of me. He turned so he could face me.

I shrugged. "I guess I needed a place to think."

"Well, this is a great place for that."

I watched him for a minute and then blurted out, "Why would you settle here in Oakdale as a preacher of all things? Couldn't you be a coach or a news caster? Why a preacher?"

He rubbed his chin. "I could've. I didn't want to. I've lived that life, Ethan. It's empty. God gave me a calling. I'm doing this because He asked me to do it."

I snorted. "How do you know God asked you to? You probably imagined it."

"I see." He nodded his head slowly. "You aren't a believer?"

"Uh, no. When I was little, I thought I believed. Then I realized what all this God stuff is really about." I motioned the church. "It's a lie to make people feel better about their crappy lives. Pray to God. He'll listen. He'll make it better, but the truth is, He isn't listening because He's not real."

"Okay, if you feel that way, why are you here? What drew you in?"

I sighed and ran my hands through my hair. "It's been a rough week. I had an accident and a girl I know from school is hurt pretty bad. When I was little, this was the church I attended. She and I knew each other then."

"Is it Emma?"

"Yeah." I looked at the floor. "She's getting worse. I'm scared she's not going to make it."

"So you came here to remember that time in your life?"

I nodded. "When I was little, my parents brought me here. Emma and I went to Sunday school together. I was out driving, trying to clear my head, and I ended up here. I haven't been inside in over ten years."

"Do you think it's simply by chance that you ended up here today?"

"What else could it be?"

"I don't know. Maybe God nudged you to come here today." He watched as I rolled my eyes. "Okay, so if it was chance, why did you come inside?"

"Honestly? I have no idea. I guess it's because I feel so freaking guilty. I didn't want Emma to get hurt and I don't know how to help her."

"You could pray."

"Prayer doesn't work." I rolled my shoulders. "I don't believe in God anymore." I waved my hand at the walls of the sanctuary. "I sit here and look at these pictures of Jesus and all I feel is anger. He's never once stepped in and helped me. My mom died a horrible death. My dad might as well be dead. He works all the time. When he's home he drinks too much and hides in his den resenting me because I'm still here and she's gone. I don't get it though. If God's real and Emma is such a big believer, you'd think He'd heal her.

Jason leaned closer to me and asked, "If God were real, what would you say to Him? Right now, if He was in this room? What would you tell Him?"

I leaned back against the pew. "I would tell Him, He sucks. I would tell Him that His timing is lousy and He might as well not show up at all."

"Ok, and what if after you told Him that, He told you that it was okay, He still loves you anyway. That He sent His son to go to the cross for you so you could tell Him those things and by grace He would forgive you if you asked?"

Jason looked around the church. "Can't you feel something bigger than yourself in this room? I can. He's here. He's listening and He wants to know you, Ethan. Faith isn't about what we can see and touch. Faith is about trusting that even when times are tough, and they will be tough, He's with us working through us."

"So you're saying my mom died for a reason? That Emma's in a coma for a reason? I don't buy it." I stood up. I wasn't up for this heavy debate. My whole body felt twitchy and anxious. I wanted out of here in a big way. It had been a mistake to come. I was never going to forgive God for letting my mom die. "I think life sucks, people let you down, they die, and if you aren't tough, you're going to get stepped on. Religion is for the weak."

Jason stood up and faced me. "Knowing God isn't about religion. Knowing God is a personal choice. Have you asked Him to show you His reasons? Have you tried to search out what you could give back to the world because of what happened? Or did you let it be the opportunity the enemy needed to alienate you from the God who could heal your pain? Has your life without God been better? Are you happy? Fulfilled? If you are so strong, you need to ask yourself some hard questions and see where the answers take you."

"Whatever." I snapped holding up my hand for him to stop talking. "I've heard enough. You sound just like Emma and Danny and all their freak friends. Jesus this, Jesus that. I just don't buy into it."

"I'm sorry to hear that Ethan. I don't think you are being entirely honest with yourself. I think you came here for a reason today. I think God is at work in your life. He's trying to get your attention. Don't be too stubborn to see what He's got planned. Trust me, I spent a lot of time chasing things that didn't matter and living a life I was ashamed of. He pulled me out of the gutter. He can open your eyes too. I'm here if you need to talk."

I didn't know how to respond, so I just nodded and walked out the door. I couldn't handle any more talk about God.

CHAPTER SIX

When I got home, no one was there. I turned on some lights and made a peanut butter sandwich. Part of me was glad that Dad wasn't there. I wasn't ready to face him yet. I grabbed my sandwich and a pop and went upstairs to my room.

I propped myself up in bed with my tablet and started surfing the Internet. I went to the usual spots, checked everyone's statuses, looked at some sports clips, and then wasted time watching stupid pet videos, all to try and distract myself.

Half an hour later, irritated, I shut the tablet off, and scooted down until I was lying flat on the bed. I lifted my left arm and draped it over my eyes to block out the light of the setting sun.

I must have fallen asleep pretty fast. It was pitch dark when I woke up a few hours later. Rolling over I opened my eyes. I could feel the presence of someone else in the room. I jerked upright and looked around. Emma sat in the window seat with her knees drawn up to her chest. She looked out over the backyard.

I watched her for a minute. Her face looked so serious and sad. I realized there was a part of me that was glad to see her, and that surprised me. The sudden onset of emotion caused me to speak a little harsher than I meant to. "What are you doing here again?"

Emma turned her head to look at me. She sighed. "It's nice to see you to Ethan."

"Sorry." I replied as I ran my hands through my hair, "I didn't mean to sound so nasty. It's just not every day I wake up to find someone in my room. Let alone…"

"Someone like me?" She finished my sentence. She turned away from the window and swung her legs to the floor and looked at me from across the room.

I glanced at the clock by my bed it read 11:33pm. Emma moved across the room and stood beside the bed. Her eyes didn't have the same sparkle I remembered. She looked tired and more faded than before.

"You okay, Emma?"

"You care?" She quipped.

"I know you have pneumonia now on top of the accident injuries."

"Yeah, it's not looking so good for me is it?" She shrugged, "I'm not worried. You shouldn't be either. Either way, I'll be fine."

"Don't talk like that Emma. You're going to be fine."

"Am I?" She folded her arms and rubbed her hands against her arms. "Because you're worried about me or because you're afraid if I die you might get charged with manslaughter?"

Guilt washed over me. "Come on, Emma. I'll admit I've been hard on you, but to want you dead? Even I'm not that big of a jerk."

"Hmm." She responded.

I swung my legs over the side of the bed and planted them on the floor. "So what are we doing tonight? Why are you here?"

She sighed. "Since my first two trips didn't have much effect, tonight I'm pulling out the big guns."

"What does that mean?"

"You'll see." She motioned toward me. "Come on, let's go already. We have a lot of ground to cover and not much time to do it."

I stood up and looked down at her upturned face. "I'm not going to like this am I?"

"Probably not, but it's something you have to do."

She reached out and took my hand. A light electrical current ran up my arm and throughout my body. I couldn't really feel her, not as if she were truly standing in front of me. The feeling felt more like a light pressure than a grip. Before I had a chance to comment, I felt a surge of energy go through my entire body. I sucked in my breath, and when I let it back out, we were standing in the cafeteria in broad daylight in the middle of a school day.

There were kids milling around talking, eating, and laughing. Emma started walking toward the windows on the far side of the room. There was a large group of kids gathered around a big oval table. It was the crowd I ran with: Ava, her friend Jenni, Grady, Tommy, his girlfriend Niki, and Jesse. I sat perched in the center of the group. Even though I'd seen other versions of myself, it was still unsettling. I could see the other me, laughing, telling a joke. He had no idea I was even in the room.

I noticed everyone had on shorts, sandals, and t-shirts. I glanced at Emma, "Is this the future?"

She nodded her head. "Yes. This is what will be if you don't make some serious changes."

I rolled my eyes. "Scare tactics?"

"Nope. No scare tactics. Just cold, hard reality."

I crossed my arms and walked a little closer to the group. "Well, it doesn't look so bad." I shrugged watching the other me hold court in the cafeteria. It was the same scene that been playing out for the last several years.

I started to make a snarky comment when movement at the door of the cafeteria caught my eye. I glanced over and then did a double take as Danny Phillips entered the room. He was completely covered in blue paint. His face, hands, clothes, every part of him was doused in electric blue. He paused in the doorway and looked around the room.

His eyes landed on the table where I sat with my friends. As he stared at us, you could feel anger coming off of him in waves. His fists opened and closed at his sides. He started to move across the room toward my table.

He crossed the room in jerky, uneven steps almost as if he were forcing himself to make the trip.

Fourth Down with Everything to Lose

As he approached I could hear the other version of me talking. He laughed and flailed his arms, exclaiming in a high girly voice, "Don't do it Ethan! How will I get it out of my clothes and my hair…" Slowly it dawned on me that the fact that Danny was doused in blue paint was no accident.

Danny made his way over, leaving a trail of blue paint in his path. Quiet fell over the cafeteria as the other kids stopped what they were doing to watch the drama about to unfold before them. He stopped in front of the table.

The other me threw his head back, pointed, and laughed, "Look, its Brainy Smurf."

Grady and Jesse covered their mouths to hide their amusement. Tommy slapped his leg and howled with laughter at the site of Danny dripping in paint.

Danny shoved his hands into the pockets of his ruined hoodie. He drew in a deep breath and pulled out his right hand. He held a gun.

One of the kids at a table somewhere across the room yelled, "Oh my God, he's got a gun." Kids started to run for the doors. Jenni jumped up, Danny swung the gun in her direction and pulled the trigger. A deafening blast filled the room and Jenni went down in a heap on the floor. Screams erupted as everyone panicked.

Danny waved the gun at the other me and screamed. "This is all your fault. I would never have hurt anyone if you hadn't kept pushing and pushing. Everything will be better when you and your psycho friends are gone. I'm not going to stand by and let you do this to other people. Someone has to stop you. All of you!"

The other me looked scared for the first time. He held his hands up and fumbled to find words to talk Danny down.

"Whoa, dude. Don't do this! Put the gun down. Let us go. You need help. You're sick."

Tears streamed down Danny's face. "No, I'm not! You're the one that's sick. You hurt people, ruin their lives, and no one holds you accountable. That's about to change."

He aimed the gun at Grady and pulled the trigger. Then he shot Louis, Jesse and Ava in quick succession. Then he leveled the gun at the other me and pulled the trigger.

I literally felt as if someone shot me with a 1,000 volts of electricity. I felt the bullet slam into my chest. Pain ripped through every part of my body. I watched the other me jerk upright upon impact and then sag forward. Blood began to soak through his shirt.

I staggered back. I could feel the fear and pain coursing through his body. I gasped for air. I could feel his, my, life slowly drain away. I watched as Danny then turned and faced the few remaining kids in the room. He held the gun up and shouted. "It's over! You don't have to live in fear anymore." He shoved the gun in his pocket and walked back across the room and out of the cafeteria.

I looked back over at the other me. His hand twitched at his side as he tried to sit up. Unable to stop the inevitable, his body went limp and the blood that soaked the front and back of his shirt slowed until it stopped.

As he died, I felt an odd sensation under my feet. The floor began to shake. It began to crumble away around my feet. I screamed as I fell through the floor.

As I fell, my body pushed through layer after layer starting with the basement of the school then through the earth down into the sewer tunnels, and then it was simply earth that continued to drop away from me. I felt as if I was falling down a huge laundry chute straight to the middle of the earth.

I continued to fall for what seemed like forever, but was probably just several seconds. I finally stopped falling and hit solid ground. I landed on my feet and fell to my knees. Shaken, I stood slowly to my feet. I found myself in a large empty room. The walls were made of packed dirt. The smell of dirt and bugs filled my nose. Somewhere in the distance I could hear water dripping.

Fear swept over me. The hair on the back of my neck stood up. Every flight or fight instinct I ever had urged me to run. I had no idea where I was, but I knew with every fiber of my being I didn't want to be here. I tried to take a step, but my legs wouldn't move. My feet felt rooted to the floor.

"Well, well, well, Ethan Morgan. We finally meet."

My head snapped up at the sound of the voice. I could make out a shape across the cavernous room, but I couldn't make out who it was.

"Do I know you?" I shouted trying to get a better look.

"Indeed, you do. And you are about to get to know me even better." The form shifted and started to move toward me. A sick feeling of dread filled me. I didn't want to see this thing whatever it was, I didn't want this to be real. I looked around frantically for Emma. If she was here then maybe it was part of the hallucination or dream. I couldn't see her in the dim light.

The thing laughed a low chuckle. "She's not welcome here. But you, Ethan, I have a special place for you here. It's a pity the kid got jumpy and killed you so young. Just think of all the incredible work I could have done through you." It clucked its tongue, "Tsk, tsk. Oh well, what's done is done and now your mine."

"Who are you?" I choked. The effort to move my lips was monumental. I felt as if someone had put weights on my tongue.

It laughed and walked closer. When it stepped into the small sliver of light surrounding me, I jerked back and let out a gasp.

Hollywood could never create something this terrifying. He had the face of a man and the body of a lizard. His face was handsome in a Johnny Depp kind of way. He had short dark hair, flawless skin, and light brown eyes that glowed. The rage that emanated from his eyes made it really hard to look directly at him.

His body was a cross between a dinosaur and a bird. He had a long torso with long arms and two back legs. He had scales where skin should have been and he had a long tail that swept out behind him. The sides of his tail had spikes coming out of it.

In his left hand he held a staff with some kind of skull on the end. His lips formed a cold, cruel smile that made the room feel like ice. The talon on his first finger on his left hand clicked against the staff as he stared at me and let me assess him.

When he saw my disgust he threw back his head and laughed. "Your response is truly priceless. Humans are always so surprised with my appearance. What did you expect? A Snake? Maybe Al Pacino with a pitchfork? " His eyes flashed and spit flew out of the corner of his mouth as he snapped. "I was a sight to behold back in the day. One day, my glory will be restored and you'll see who I really am."

In my heart I knew who this was, but my mind was still fighting the reality of what I was seeing. I have never experienced fear like this before. He was mesmerizing and repulsive at the same time.

He rolled his eyes. "Cat got your tongue? Are you going to pretend you don't know who I am?" He waved his staff at me. "Fine with me. You'll bow to me soon enough." He leaned in toward me and sniffed. "Ahhhhh, I never get tired of the smell of fear."

I wanted to run away from him or at least back up a few steps but I couldn't, all I could do was stand there as he started to walk around me in a tight circle. I felt like a cow being led to the slaughter. He made his way slowly all the way around me. He stopped in front of me and narrowed his eyes and poked me with the staff. "You aren't dead. What game is He playing?"

He cocked his head, pointing his ear to the ceiling as if he were listening to someone. A deep, angry, hiss spewed out of his mouth. "No way! He's mine! He's been mine for ten years! You can't do this!" He screeched and hissed flailing his arms and the staff. At the ceiling.

He whirled back around and glared at me. "This isn't over boy. I will have my flesh. You can't escape me!"

A voice came out of nowhere, "Back off, you know the rules."

My eyes darted to find the source of the voice. Emma stood off to the side of the room. She had her arms crossed and fire in her eyes. The weird bluish green light was back. It surrounded her entire body in a mist.

He growled at her and waved his arms frantically. "Go on then. Get him out of here. I don't know what kind of game He's playing but get out of here or all bets are off." He looked me in the eye and gave me an icy smile. "I haven't lost you yet." Then he leaned in close to my face, ran his finger down my cheek, and whispered in a bone chilling voice, "I'll be seeing you again, Ethan Morgan."

……..

I jerked my head back and found myself suddenly standing in a long hallway. I looked around frantically to see if he was still there. Thankfully, he was nowhere in sight. I blew out a long breath I hadn't realized I was holding and rubbed my chest to calm my pounding heart.

Emma stood off to my left. She was staring at something with an intent expression. I turned my head to see what she was looking at and noticed for the first time we weren't alone. Thick steel bars divided off several portions of the room into square cells. I counted six cells lining the hallway on both sides of the aisle where we stood.

I noticed someone seated on the bottom bunk of the second cell. He sat slumped forward with his head in his hands. I took a tentative step forward to get a better look. His hair was in his face and his body was rocking back and forth. Gut wrenching sobs and deep sorrowful moans echoed off the walls in the room around us.

He raised his head and I jumped back. It was Danny. He clutched a crumpled up piece of newspaper in his right hand. I could still see patches of faded blue paint on his hands and under his fingernails.

I wanted to see what he was holding so I stepped up to the bars. I reached out to grasp them, but instead of touching metal my hands slid right through the bars. I looked back at Emma, she waved her hand toward Danny, "He can't see you, Ethan. You can come and go. He won't know you're here."

I sucked in my breath and took a step forward, pressing my body up against the bars. A tingling sensation buzzed through me. Afraid to stop I pushed forward and found myself on the other side, inside the cell.

I held up hands up in front of my face. "Cool." I muttered.

Dropping my hands, I took a couple of steps closer to Danny and glanced down at the paper he held in his fist. The headline read, "When Bullying Leads to Murder..."

Danny slowly lifted his head and looked out toward the front of the cell. His eyes were flat and lifeless.

He drew in a shaky breath and stood slowly to his feet. Still clutching the paper, he began to pace back and forth in front of the bunk. His lips twitched as he muttered, "Abomination. I'm an abomination. If only they'd left me alone. I didn't have a choice. I had to stop them." He looked up at the ceiling and cried out. "I couldn't wait on you, God! I had to get justice. Justice for Emma, for myself, for everyone they've destroyed." His hands moved to crush the paper into a ball. He threw it against the wall and screamed. "It could've ended differently if you had just shown up!"

Emma walked into the cell the same way I had, and joined me to watch Danny pace and talk to himself. Obviously he had experienced some kind of psychotic break. He continued to babble, pace, and rub his cheeks with clenched fists. He didn't look anything like the same kid I had picked on over the years. He looked...crazy and pathetic.

I looked over at Emma. "What happened?"

I noticed for the first time that she was crying. She wiped her eyes and sighed. "After he shot you and your friends, he walked out of the school in a daze. The police found him wandering around in the park completely detached from reality, mumbling about the school being free. They found the gun in his pocket and arrested him. He's been here since they found him.

I looked back at Danny. This was the guy who had walked into a cafeteria full of teenagers, pulled out a gun, and proceeded to shoot me and my close friends. Logically, I knew I should be angry at him, bitter, and full of hate for what he'd done. But I didn't feel any of those things. Instead, my heart felt heavy.

All the times that I had teased him, embarrassed him, and sometimes even humiliated him had broken him down until he felt as if he had nothing to lose. My face flamed with shame. Suddenly none of it seemed funny anymore. My eyes burned from tears that threatened to fall. I swallowed hard and pushed them down.

Danny came to a standstill in the middle of his cell. He was still mumbling, but his voice was so low I couldn't tell what he was saying. Suddenly he cocked his head to the side as if he was listening to someone. He slowly nodded his head as if he were agreeing with whomever he heard.

In the blink of an eye he straightened up and the confusion left his eyes. A tiny half smile lifted the corners of his mouth. I felt the hair on the back of my neck stand up. A dark presence seeped into the cell. Fear spread through the room until it reached every crevice.

"Oh no." I muttered looking around frantically. Hadn't I just escaped that same cold, hate filled fear? My eyes flew to the end of the hall. A tall, dark form emerged and began to glide toward us.

My eyes flew back to Danny. His eyes were fixed on the figure. I reached out to grab his arm to try and shake some sense into him. "Danny, no! Don't listen to him! You've got to snap out of this." Each time I tried to grab his arm, my hands just slid right through him.

I searched frantically around the cell for Emma, "Emma, what's going on? I thought we were done with him?"

Emma stood rooted to the floor her eyes wide with sadness. She shook her head. "Not yet."

"Can't you do something?"

She shook her head, "Not this time."

The thing I had just escaped from stopped at the door of the cell and winked at me. I recoiled in disgust. "Good work, kid." He eyed Danny with a smile of satisfaction on his face.

"This one isn't getting away." He flicked his staff in Danny's direction. A deep hiss erupted from the end and a thick, dark mist swirled out of the staff. It moved with precision across the room and slammed into Danny's chest disappearing inside of his body.

He didn't seem to feel whatever it was, but it sparked him to move. He made his way back to the bunk and knelt down and fumbled around under the mattress. After a few seconds he seemed to find what he was looking for and got back to his feet.

I strained to see what he was holding in his hand. It was short, rusty and jagged. My eyes flew open wide and I leaped forward to stop him. I stumbled as my hands went through his body and I found myself sprawled on the floor looking up. Danny brought the makeshift knife up to his throat. He drew in a deep breath and muttered, "I'm all alone now. No one can save me."

I fumbled around trying to get my feet underneath me and get up off the floor. Tears streamed down my cheeks, "Come on, don't do this, Danny!" I sobbed.

He jabbed the makeshift knife into his throat. He must have hit an artery because almost immediately dark red blood began spurting out. His hand flew to his neck and he staggered forward a couple of steps, then he sagged to the floor in slow motion. Blood gushed out of the wound and poured through his fingers. He fell on his side and started to convulse. His body jerked and sputtered as he tried to breathe through the blood that was coming out of his nose and mouth. He began to cough uncontrollably. Blood splattered everywhere. I knelt by his side and tried to cover the wound with my hand but my efforts were useless. My hands just kept going through him. He convulsed a few more times and then his body went limp. I looked from him to Emma, her arms were wrapped around her waist and tears coursed down her cheeks.

The sound of a deep chuckle reminded me we weren't alone. I jerked my head back to glare at him. The sound of his laughter was like nails on a chalkboard. He reached out and stomped the staff on the ground. The dark mist rolled out of Danny's body and went back into the staff.

The thing called out, "Danny. It's time." Right in front of me, Danny stood up out of his body and stared at the thing calling him. I watched as he stepped away from his own body, his shoulders hunched, eyes cast down, as if he had no will of his own, he walked to the front of the cell. He moved through the bars and stood in front of the thing.

With the wave of a hand, shackles snapped onto Danny's wrists and ankles. They started down the hall. I tried to go after them, but they dissolved into the wall and I was left staring at cold, gray concrete.

My entire body felt sore as if I'd just played eight quarters of football back to back. I looked back at Emma. She had her back to me. Her shoulders shook. I knew she was crying.

I moved across the room to her side. "Emma, this isn't real, is it? It hasn't happened yet. You are just showing me this to scare me." I tried to grab her arm, my hand just passed through her, frustrated I yelled, "Please tell me this isn't real! Tell me there's time to change it!"

She pulled away from me and walked a few feet away and turned to face me. "I honestly don't know. I think there's a chance this could all happen. A very real chance. You've done so much damage. Danny struggles with anger toward you and your friends. He has tried to find peace, but you won't let him. I don't know what he's capable of, especially…"

"Especially if you die?" I finished for her.

She nodded her head. "Yeah, I think my death may be too much for him."

I ran my hand through my hair. "I don't know how to stop this, Emma. I'm lost."

Emma back over to where I stood. She stopped in front of me and looked up. Her eyes searched mine as she spoke. "There's only one way Ethan."

Emotions I hadn't acknowledged in years started to surface. The pain I had caused, the anger over my mother's death and my dad's inability to move on all rose up to the surface and overwhelmed me.

Tears welled up in my eyes. A deep sadness choked me as sobs started to wrack my body. I crumpled to the cold floor in the jail cell beside Danny's lifeless body. Years and years of pain, frustration, and anger poured out. I muttered the words, "What have I become?' over and over until my body was limp from exhaustion.

CHAPTER SEVEN

I jerked awake. My eyes searched the room, no Emma. I was alone. Heaviness settled on me as I remembered everything in vivid detail from the night before. Being shot, going to hell, the devil, Danny's suicide, all of it was fresh in my mind. Had it been a dream?

It was real. It changed everything. Did I believe in God again? I wasn't entirely sure. I'd witnessed some powerful things the night before. If I believed the creature I'd seen had been Satan, then God and Jesus had to be real too. I wondered briefly if my mind was playing tricks on me. I shook my head. I knew full well what had happened was not all in my head.

I glanced at the clock it read 8:45am. A sense of urgency came over me. I sat up and swung my legs over the side of the bed. I suddenly felt a huge need to apologize and make things right.

My stomach turned at the thought. If what had happened the night before was any indication, I was the last person Danny would want to talk to much less accept an apology from and frankly, I couldn't remember the last time I'd apologized for anything.

I got ready as quietly as I could and snuck out of the house. I left a note for my dad and headed to my old church.

When I arrived, the street was lined with cars. People stood outside on the front stoop laughing and greeting each other. I found a parking space off to the side on an adjacent street.

I turned my truck off and sat there afraid to get out and go inside. Fear reared its ugly head and made me question my decision to attend. What would everyone say? Would I be welcome? I decided to wait in my truck until the service started. That way I could avoid a lot of conversation. The urgency I'd been experiencing was getting stronger. Finally, a few minutes past ten, I heard the band start to play. Drawing in a deep breath, I climbed out of my truck, wiped my sweaty palms on my pants, and walked up to the door.

It was now or never. My hand shook as I reached out and pulled open the door.

When I walked inside the sound of the praise band washed over me. I felt a calm presence surround me as I slipped into a pew in the back of the church. Other than a couple of people who turned their heads to see who had walked in, everyone seemed absorbed in the music and didn't notice one more teenager in the back.

I looked around the sanctuary and saw a lot of people I knew and some I hadn't seen in over ten years. My eyes landed on Danny, he stood in the middle of a group of teenagers. When I saw him my heart lurched in my chest. He didn't look homicidal or suicidal, but I knew what I had witnessed the night before and I knew what I needed to do.

I was surprised when I found the service moving. Hearing the songs, and listening as Jason spoke about adversity, our desire for everything to go perfectly, and what happens when it doesn't. There were several moments during the sermon when I felt as if he was speaking directly to me.

Toward the end of the service, we all bowed our heads and reflected on what he'd just preached. My heart ached. I suddenly couldn't wait to talk to Danny. He had to know I was sorry. Somehow, I had to make it right.

When the sermon ended I waited a couple of minutes as everyone gathered their things and headed for the doors. Part of me wanted to walk out with them. Maybe it would be good enough that I came today. I felt a nudge inside, I knew it wasn't enough to just show up. I had to apologize and start making things right. I gave myself a mental shake and went to find Danny.

I found him standing off to the side of the stage area with a couple of other kids. A flush crept up my cheeks; they were all kids I had tormented at one time or another. This was going to be a lot harder than I expected. As I approached the group, one of the smaller kids noticed me. His eyes flew open and his jaw dropped. Several other kids turned to see what had caused him so much surprise. As soon as they saw me, they fell silent and stared at me.

Danny crossed his arms and glared at me. I gave the group a slight nod, "Hey Danny. Everyone." It occurred to me I had no idea what their names were.

Danny lifted his right eyebrow. "Ethan." He watched me for several seconds while I fumbled with how to even start, "Did you want something?" he asked.

I nodded my head and cleared my throat. "Uh, yeah. Is there someplace we can go and talk?"

He snorted. "Are you kidding? I wouldn't be alone with you even if you offered to pay me. Say what you have to say and let me get back to my friends."

I lifted my hands in surrender. "I totally deserve that, but I'm not here to cause trouble. I'm here to…. apologize."

"Seriously?" One of the other kids squeaked.

I gave him an irritated glance and looked back at Danny. "Yeah, seriously. If you'll just give me a few minutes, I will explain everything. You have my word in front of your friends that I won't do anything to embarrass or hurt you. I just want to talk."

He looked uneasy, but shrugged, "Okay, but if something happens to me, there are a lot of witnesses."

"Not a problem."

"Okay." He looked at the other kids. "Hey guys, if you don't hear from me in an hour or so, send out a search party."

They all bobbed their heads in agreement. We started for the door. As we got closer, Jason stepped away from a young couple and grabbed Danny's arm. "Hey guys, how's it going?" His voice was friendly but his eyes searched our faces. "Everything okay?"

Danny shrugged. "I guess so."

I gave Jason a slight smile. "I hope so. I came to the service this morning to apologize to Danny."

Jason rocked back on his heels and looked back and forth between us, "Is that so? Well, then don't let me get in the way." He reached out with his hand and squeezed my shoulder. "I'm glad you came back today. Apologizing is never easy, but I think you'll be surprised by the peace you'll feel when you're done."

"Thank you. I hope so."

"Alright, off you go. Let me know if either of you need anything."

Danny and I proceeded out the doors of the church, down the street, and climbed into my old pick up. Danny gripped the door handle with his hand and leaned heavily against the door.

I put the key in the ignition and turned toward him, "Look, I promise, I'm serious about not hurting you or doing anything stupid. You can relax a little."

"You'll forgive me if I have my doubts," Danny chirped from his corner of the cab.

"Where do you want to go?" I asked as I started the truck.

"Uh, I don't know if I should go anywhere with you. Alone."

"Point taken. How about we go to your house? That way you'll have home field advantage? Plus when we're done, you'll already be home."

"Okay, I guess."

"Great, where do you live?" Another testament to how oblivious I was in regards to other people.

He gave me directions. We drove in silence. He finally motioned me into the drive way of a large, navy blue house with dark gray shutters.

We got out of the truck and went inside. The inside was as immaculate as the outside. Wood floors gleamed in the early afternoon sun, antiques were positioned around the lower level, and the walls were painted a soft cream.

"Nice house." I commented.

"Thanks." Danny replied. He motioned toward the staircase. "My room is upstairs."

He stopped outside his room and gave me a weak smile, "I wasn't expecting company."

I shrugged. "No worries. I have football gear all over my room. It's cool."

He opened the door and stepped inside. "Come on in."

His room was a lot like mine. A big queen size bed filled most of the space. He had a built-in desk and shelves in one corner and a big window beside his bed. It was messy with the typical stuff, books, clothes, posters, game controllers, but nothing out of the ordinary.

He walked over and pulled the desk chair closer to the bed and motioned for me to sit down. He sat on the edge of the bed facing me.

I sat down on the chair, suddenly very uncomfortable. Now what? I was here, facing him. What in the world did I say?

He cocked his head and raised his eyebrow, "Well?"

"I know." I let out a nervous laugh. "I don't apologize a whole lot."

"Imagine that," Danny snorted.

"Okay, here goes…" I took a deep breath and looked him in the eyes. "I'm sorry for what a total jerk I've been to you and your friends. I've been pretty awful."

"A tooth ache is awful. You are a living nightmare."

"Fair enough. I am a nightmare. There is no excuse for my behavior. I let a really personal tragedy make me into someone I don't want to be."

"Why the sudden light bulb moment?" Danny asked.

"Well, if I tell you, you may think I'm crazy."

"I doubt anything you say could make my opinion of you any worse."

I gave a short laugh. "You aren't going to make this easy are you?"

"Should I?"

"Probably not." I agreed. I rubbed my hands on my knees and looked him in the eyes. "Okay, here goes. The past few days have been like something out of a movie. It all started when Emma…"

He interrupted me, "What's Emma got to do with this?"

"I'm getting to that. Hold on to your seat Danny, I have something pretty incredible to tell you."

……..

As I talked, Danny's face changed emotions almost as fast as I could complete sentences. At first, he sat on the bed, his arms crossed, eye brows lifted, scowl firmly in place. The more I told him about what had happened with Emma, the subsequent visits, and the changes I was going through, his hands fell to the top of the bed. His eyes became teary and his adam's apple bobbed like a buoy in the lake.

I paused when I reached the part about my journey through my own death, hell, and his suicide. I wanted to give him time to absorb what I had said before I really threw him a curve ball.

He shook his head, "This is crazy Ethan. Are you really telling me that Emma has been appearing to you and taking you on trips while she's lying in a coma?"

I nodded vigorously. "That's exactly what I'm telling you."

"And, you are also admitting you were tormenting her on the night of the accident?"

I looked down at my hands, "Yeah. Not my finest moment."

Danny blew out a long breath. "I knew she didn't just wreck her bike. Why did you chase her like that?"

I shrugged, "I was mad, ready for a fight, and she was there." I watched him process everything.

"I don't know, Ethan, it's awfully farfetched. Are you just trying to get out of trouble or ease your conscious?"

"That's what I thought originally, but it keeps happening. And, Danny, I swear it's real. It's the most vivid dreams, hallucinations, whatever you want to call them that I've ever experienced."

"It's crazy alright. It's just your word until she wakes up. Why not keep your mouth shut?"

I cleared my throat. "Because I owe it to her. I owe it to you and everyone I've been a jerk too. I can't stay quiet anymore.

And, it's not just my word. When I tell you the last part, the most recent part, I think it will be the confirmation you need to know it's real."

"What's the last part?" Danny asked, crossing his legs and propping his head in his hands. His eyes locked on me, waiting.

When I finished telling him about the shooting, hell, and his dying he simply sat on the end of the bed and stared at something behind my head. He didn't move and he didn't say anything. After several long minutes, I leaned forward and asked, "Danny, are you okay?"

He finally blinked several times, cleared his throat, and looked at me. His eyes were wide and a small trickle of sweat ran down the side of his face. "How do you know?" He whispered, his voice catching.

I shrugged. "Know what? I didn't know anything until Emma showed me."

He moved slowly untangling his arms and legs and stood to his feet. He moved past me to his desk and picked up a black book. He came back and sank down on the bed. The book was a bible. He opened it and riffled through the pages until he found what he was looking for. With shaky hands, he pulled out a folded piece of paper and handed it to me.

"Here's your confirmation." His eyes wouldn't meet mine as he pushed the folded paper toward me.

I took it in my hands and gently unfolded the paper. It was worn as if it had been folded and unfolded many times. When I got it open, I looked at the writing. It was a list of names. My name was at the top. Several of my closest friends were listed as well. There were about ten names on the paper. In the margins there were images sketched that included guns, tombstones, people crying, people cheering. As I looked over the paper it slowly dawned on me what I was looking at. My eyes flew to Danny's face. He looked away from me and stared out the window.

"What is this, Danny? Is it what I think it is?"

He nodded slowly. "Two years ago, before Emma and I became good friends, I was a different person. I hated you and your friends. You had made my life a living hell. One day in study hall, right after you had pants me in front of the girls' locker room, I made a list." He pointed at the paper. "That list. I began to fantasize about what it would feel like to stand up to you and your friends. From there it blossomed into the idea of making you stop for good. I became obsessed with ways to kill you. Every time you did something awful, I plotted."

"Why haven't you done it?" I asked, somewhat afraid of the answer.

He gave a laugh. "Because of Emma. One day in the library, the paper fell out of my book bag. She picked it up. She knew right away what it was. She begged me to come to church with her and talk to the youth pastor. She said if I didn't go, she would have to report me." He smiled. "She's stubborn like that. Even when I told her I would add her to the list, she didn't budge. She just kept at me. So I went to church with her. The youth pastor and I had some long talks, we prayed together, and about two weeks after Emma found out my secret, I gave my life to Jesus."

There was that name again. I shifted in my chair. "Did Jesus make you not want to kill me?"

"Yes and no." Danny, shifted on the bed. He scratched his head, "Having Jesus in my life has given me incredible freedom and peace. He has changed just about everything in my life." He pointed to the paper, "I keep that list as a reminder of what I was capable of and what I never want to happen."

"But I saw you do it. Emma showed me what would happen if I didn't change and she dies. You go through with it. You kill me and several other people." I looked at the list in my hand. I held the proof that it was all real. Emma's visits. Jesus. Hell. Satan. All of it…real. Emotions began to well up inside me. I looked at Danny, he was watching me closely.

He rubbed his hands together and sighed. "I don't know, Ethan. Maybe her death would have been the final straw. I've been angry at you for a long time. I'd like to tell you I would never snap and hurt anyone but, honestly, I don't know. I have spent a lot of time praying about my anger. If Emma dies, I would lose my best friend and spiritual mentor. She's shown me Jesus like no one else. The thought of her dying makes me physically sick. I know she'd go to heaven, but what about me? I would miss her."

I flopped back in my chair and stared at Danny. "Honestly, Danny, through all of this, I've never given your pain a second thought. I'm really sorry I hurt your best friend. Emma used to be my friend too, but it was a long time ago."

"Thanks." He blew out a deep breath and smiled at me, "I think you coming here today may have changed the future." Danny reached over and gripped my shoulder. "We need to ask ourselves, how do we let God use this situation to change us? Do we keep going on our paths and destroy each other, or do we ask Jesus in to our lives and ask Him to change us? You coming to church today and apologizing was a huge step in the right direction. Were you serious about wanting to change?"

Tears slid down my cheeks. I whispered, "Yes, I want to change. I don't want to be this person anymore, but I don't know how. I've done some pretty horrible things. How could God ever love me and forgive me?"

Danny squeezed my shoulder. "Dude that's the best part. Jesus already loves you. He just wants you to love him back. He wants to love you, all of you. Warts and all. If you wait until you think you deserve forgiveness, you'll never get it. I'm a great example of that. Planning a murder isn't exactly Christ-like behavior."

I stared at him, scared out of my mind. There was a time when I thought I was a Christian, but, honestly, I had no idea what it meant to follow Jesus. A relationship? That sounded scary.

"What if I fail? What if I screw up again?"

"Oh, it's not if, it's when. You will screw up, but that's where grace comes in. You've got to ask forgiveness and move on. Once you really know Jesus, you'll find yourself wanting to do the right thing more and more." He leaned back and smiled the first real smile I'd seen from him. "This is so cool. God sure knows what He's doing doesn't He? He's used Emma to try and reach you before its too late and He used her to remind me why Jesus is so important and what He's done for me. This is amazing."

I nodded my head. I still wasn't sure about the whole "being saved thing." I stood, "I better go. I meant what I said, I am sorry for what I've done. I'll leave you and all of your friends alone from now on. I promise."

Danny leaped up. "Ethan, come to youth group tonight! Please. I think it'll help you. Don't wait another day to say yes to Jesus. What do you say?"

I snorted. "If you'd asked me a week ago to come to youth group I would have had some choice words to say and maybe a punch or two to throw."

"And today?"

I sighed, "I'm considering it."

Danny laughed and slapped my back. "Awesome. I hope I see you there tonight." He reached out and hugged me. I froze. He pulled back and chuckled. "Sorry. I'm just so happy."

"Happy?" I felt as if someone had backed a tractor over my body.

"Yeah, happy. God is at work and you and I have a front row seat. How cool is that?"

CHAPTER EIGHT

I left Danny's house more confused than ever. I didn't want to go home yet. I needed some time to get my head straight. I drove through town and found myself going by the cemetery. I slowed my truck down and swung inside the wrought iron gates. I parked my truck and walked through the headstones to a gravel path.

I walked about halfway up one of the hills and stepped off the path by a big old pine tree. I stopped beside a modest headstone and stared down at it. It read:

Lisa Morgan
Mother
Wife
Friend
6/12/1961-10/13/2005

As I stared at the headstone, my legs began to feel heavy. They felt like they did after a particularly grueling football practice. I looked around and didn't see anyone, so I sank down to the ground beside her headstone.

I sat there in the stillness for a few minutes. I hadn't been here in a long time. The quiet around me felt overwhelming. Even then trees seemed to know it was a place where quiet was the rule.

I sighed, "Oh Mom. I miss you so much. Everything was different when you were alive." I wiped away tears and continued. "I guess I forgot a lot of the good times we used to have, at least until this week. I'm starting to remember them now. I got caught up in what you went through at the end and how our lives fell apart after you were gone. I let all of the good stuff get shoved in the back of my mind." I sighed heavily and plucked absently at the grass.

"You know she's not in there, don't you?"

I jerked at the sound of another person's voice. I looked up and Emma stood on the other side of mom's headstone.

I shrugged. "If you say so."

"Oh Ethan, are you still fighting what you already know is real? If you believe in God and you believe in hell, and you know your Mom was saved, then surely you know she's not in there." She pointed at the ground.

"Yeah, I know." I choked back tears. "I just miss her so much. I didn't for a long time. I was so angry at her for dying. And, if I'm being honest, not only for dying, but for dying such a painful and hideous death. I know it's not rational, but its how I felt."

"Sometimes emotions aren't rational." Emma replied as she sank down to the ground and sat across from me on the other side of mom's grave. "Do you come here a lot?"

"No." I shook my head. "I haven't been here in a long time."

"Why did you come today?"

I shrugged. "I don't know for sure. I had a really good talk with Danny. We came to an understanding. I apologized and he showed me the list."

"Ahh, the list."

"Yeah, that was a little unsettling."

"But not surprising?"

"No, not since I saw what you showed me last night. After what I've put him through over the last several years, I'm actually surprised he didn't already snap."

Emma and I sat in silence for a couple of minutes. She looked around the graveyard and then back at me. "This is my last visit."

"What? Are you going to wake up?"

She gave me a small smile. "I'm not sure. I wasn't told what would happen at the end of the five days. All I know is that I was given five days to try and change the path you were on."

"Emma, it worked. I'm different." I patted my chest and laughed. "I've changed inside. I'm not the same person I was a few days ago. I don't want to be that angry, scary person anymore. Ever."

"That's great." She nodded her head and smiled. Her smile didn't quite reach her eyes. "I'm glad it worked."

"Why do you seem sad?" I asked puzzled by the look in her eyes.

"I'm glad you're changed Ethan, I really am. But I was hoping you would go one step further and give your life to Jesus."

"I don't know Emma, the whole salvation and relationship with Jesus scares me."

"Why?"

"Can I trust Him?"

"Yes, you can trust Him. Life is hard, Ethan. He didn't promise us an easy life. He promised to see us through it."

I picked at some grass and sighed. "How will He forgive me for my doubt and anger? I feel so hopelessly unworthy."

Her smile spread from her lips to her eyes and lit up her entire face. "That's why the gospel of Jesus is so awesome. We can't be worthy. You just have to love Jesus and accept what he's done for you"

"You sound like Danny."

"He's a smart guy."

"Hmm." I replied. Everything kept coming back to Jesus. I looked over at Emma. "It's the only way isn't it?"

"Yeah, Jesus is the way, the truth and the life. We can't get to God except through him."

"I'm working on it Emma."

"I can see that. I hope you take that leap of faith Ethan. You won't be sorry." She stood up. "Well, it's time for me to go."

"Emma?" I asked as I got to my feet.

"Yes?"

"In case I don't get to tell you, thanks."

"For what?"

"Saving my life. Showing me all of this. Showing me the truth."

"That's what friends do, Ethan. They help each other, even when the other person doesn't want help."

"You are persistent." I smiled joking with her.

She started walking toward the path and called over her shoulder, "And you are incredibly stubborn."

I ran after her. She paused and looked up at me. "What is it, Ethan, I don't have much time."

I blinked back tears and tried to keep my voice from shaking. "I hope you wake up. I miss you and a lot of other people do, too. I promise you I will make this right."

She reached her hand out and patted my arm. I wished so badly I could really feel her hand and not just the sensation of her touching me. "I know you'll do the right thing, Ethan. Take care of Danny and your father. Don't let whatever happens with me take away the wonderful gift you've been given. Second chances don't come that often."

I nodded and watched as she turned and walked into the fading afternoon light. I wasn't a bit surprised when she simply disappeared into the air.

....

I got home and walked into the kitchen. I could hear the sound of the television coming from the den. I walked back to let my dad know I was home.

"Hey dad, I'm home."

He grunted an acknowledgement, so I turned to go upstairs.

"Where had you been all day? You don't usually have practice on Sundays."

My body stiffened up. The tone of his voice was rough as if he'd already had a couple of beers and was ready for a fight. I briefly debated lying to him, but a huge part of me wanted him to know what was going on. I drew in a deep breath and answered his question.

"I got up and went to church this morning. Then I went to a classmate's house to apologize for being a jerk and then I went to the cemetery and visited mom's grave. What about you? What did you do today?" I knew as I said it I was inviting a fight. My tone implied exactly what I was feeling.

"You did what?" He snapped, jumping up out of his recliner.

I held my ground, "I went to our old church."

"Why on earth would you do that? We haven't been inside a church since..." He stopped as he realized what he was about to say.

"Since mom died?" I finished for him. "High time we got back don't you think? Ten years is a long time."

The base of my dad's neck turned red and the color crawled up his face to the top of his head. "Excuse me? Who are you to tell me when it's time to do anything? I made a vow never to set foot in a church again and I intend to keep it. God didn't answer my prayers so I don't owe him a thing."

"Really? Is that how you see it?" I cocked my head and looked at him. "So because you didn't get your way, God can't be real? I don't think Mom would see it that way."

"You better shut up and get to your room. I'm not having this conversation with you. You are just a punk kid who isn't man enough to stand on his own." He waved his hand, "I've told you before, and I'll tell you again, only the weak need God to save them. I'll save myself, thank you very much."

"You've done a bang up job so far."

"What did you just say?" He took a step toward me.

I stood my ground and looked him square in the eye. "I said, you've done a bang up job. The mighty Ben Morgan doesn't need anyone or anything. I've been quiet and miserable for ten years. I'm not shutting up this time. For ten years I've done what you wanted me to do. I've gone to school, kept quiet at home, played good football, made decent grades, everything to make you notice me, and you know what? None of it worked. You've spent ten years ignoring me, throwing crumbs of affection that you thought would keep me quiet. You let our home turn into an empty house of four walls. All the love and comfort that we use to have, died the day mom died. Plus, you've undermined everything Mom taught me about Jesus and you've made God into a monster. She would hate you for that!"

"I work two jobs to keep you clothed and fed. You don't know the sacrifices I've made or the pain I've been in. You don't get to stand there and tell me what your Mom would do!" He screamed. His face was purple and his fists were clenched, but I couldn't stop myself.

"Or what? You'll watch some more television and drink some more beer? You'll come to my games ten minutes late and leave ten minutes early so you don't have to spend any time with me. I'm done with it dad. You checked out ten years ago and you've never checked back in. I've been alone for ten years. I've turned into a hateful, bitter person with no real friends and no real hope. It took someone on their deathbed to show me how much I need Jesus. He's no joke, Dad, and He's no monster. People get sick, people die. Too young and in horrible ways, but if you would have reached for Him when it happened I know He would have given you the strength to get through it. Instead, you let the enemy pull you in a pit so deep you couldn't see a way out of it. I know the sacrifices you've made and I didn't ask you to do any of it. All I've ever wanted was my dad. But that seems to be the last thing you want. I know it was a huge disappointment that Mom died of cancer instead of me. I'm truly sorry she was the one who died, because by the way you've acted all these years, you might as well be dead too."

His hand came up fast and slapped me hard across the face. I jerked back from the force. He froze as soon as he hit me realizing what he'd done. We both stared at each other for a few awkward seconds. His hand fell to his side. Anger coursed through the room. I took a step backward toward the door, and without saying a word, I walked back down the hall and out the kitchen door, letting it slam behind me.

……..

I walked into the church angry at the world. Danny ran up to me, "You came, Ethan!! I didn't know if you would."

"I said I'd think about it didn't I?" I snapped. He flinched. My stomach knotted. I reached out and grabbed his arm. "I'm sorry, Danny. I didn't mean to snap. It's been an emotional day."

He nodded a few times. "I know, it's been pretty wild. You okay? Did something happen?"

"Yeah, I went to my mom's grave and saw Emma again. She said it was the last time she would appear."

Danny's eyes flew open wide, "What do you mean?"

"I don't know, Danny. She said she's not sure if she will come back to her body or go on to heaven. "

"Wow." He muttered rubbing his eyes.

"I know. I think we all need to really pray for her."

"You're right. We need to intercede and ask God to heal her."

"I had a fight with my dad too. He didn't want me to come tonight."

"Why?"

"He's angry at God for letting my Mom die. I said some truthful things only I could have been more tactful. I was pretty brutal. I just couldn't hold it in anymore."

Danny started toward the group, "We'll pray about that too. Come on, let's get started."

All the chatter stopped as we approached the group. I was suddenly self-conscious with twelve pairs of eyes on me. Every kid in the group was someone I'd done something awful to in the past.

Danny spoke up, "Hey everyone, you probably know Ethan from school. He used to go to church here a long time ago. He's had a pretty incredible week and would like to join us tonight. Is everyone okay with that?"

Some of the kids shifted in their seats. After several awkward seconds of silence, Jason who was there leading the group smiled and answered for the group. "Absolutely. Sit down, Ethan, welcome to our group. We were just talking about forgiveness and how to extend the hand of friendship to those in need."

I smiled weakly at the group and replied, "Did you cover how to forgive when the hand of friendship was bitten off and thrown back in your face?"

Some of the kids chuckled. Jason laughed out loud, "We'll make sure to include that in our session. It's good to have you here, Ethan, seriously."

"Thank you. I'm glad to be here. Is it okay if I say something before we get started?" Jason nodded his head yes. I plowed on so I wouldn't lose my courage. "I would like to make an apology to every one of you sitting here." I made sure to make eye contact with every person in the group. "I know I have been a complete jerk and I know it's going to take time for you to trust me or believe what I'm saying, but please, I want you all to know, I am truly sorry and I want to change my life."

Jason used what I said to jump into the lesson on forgiveness. As the night wore on, more and more of the kids opened up and actually talked to me.

Toward the end of the lesson, Danny spoke up to the group. "I can't go into details, but Ethan has had a pretty incredible week involving the accident with Emma. He feels strongly we should all pray together for her healing. I'd also like to pray for Ethan and his Dad that they would be able to heal their relationship and build a better future together."

Everyone bowed their heads and we prayed. Several of the kids prayed out loud. One girl read scripture. The whole experience was incredibly moving. I swear I felt God in the room with us. As we finished the prayer, I lifted my head and with tears in my eyes said to the group, "We're not done yet, I don't want to live another minute without Him in my life. Would you all help me accept Jesus as my savior?"

Through a lot of tears, I knelt on the floor surrounded by people I had bullied and tormented and gave my life to Jesus.

CHAPTER NINE

The rowdy chorus of a rock song jerked me awake. I reached over and slapped the snooze button and rolled onto my back. I stared up at the ceiling and let my mind wander back over the last several days.

Had it really only been five days? It sure felt like a lot longer. So much had changed. I felt completely different than I had just a few days earlier. I no longer felt alone and angry. For the first time in a long time I was excited about what the day would bring, but nervous because I knew I had a lot of work to do.

I'd spent quite a bit of time the night before thinking over what I needed to do about the accident. Only Danny and I knew what had really happened. Should I go to the police and confess? Should I stay quiet and hope Emma wouldn't say anything? Was that what Jesus would do? I sighed and swung my legs over the edge of the bed.

My phone beeped. I reached over and grabbed it off the nightstand. It was a text from Ava.

"Hey, what happened to you this weekend? We need to talk."

I cringed. She was right. We did need to talk. I texted back, "How about third period?"

She answered, "Fine. See you then."

I got up and headed for the shower. Why when everything felt so new and full of possibilities did I feel such dread at making amends with the people I had wronged. It was going to be a long day.

....

A little while later, dressed and ready for school, I grabbed my backpack and jogged down the stairs, into the kitchen and right into my dad.

Shock reverberated throughout my entire body. I knew something was up. I couldn't remember the last time I beat him out the door. He had to be at the factory by 7:00am.

I mumbled "sorry" and tried to skirt around him as fast as I could. I didn't want a repeat of the day before.

"Danny." He reached out and grabbed my arm. "We need to talk."

I stopped in my tracks and lifted my eyes to his. "I thought we said it all yesterday."

"No. We didn't. Please." He motioned toward the kitchen table, "Have a seat and let's talk for a couple of minutes."

"Ok." I responded. I put my book bag down and sat in one of the chairs. He sat down across from me.

By the way his fingers drummed against the table top, I figured he was just as nervous as I was. He sighed out loud and ran his hand through his hair. "Ethan, I'm sorry."

I sat up a little straighter.

"I have been a lousy father to you. You could've been a little less harsh yesterday and I shouldn't have slapped you, but you weren't wrong in what you said. I needed to hear it. I didn't want to hear it, but I needed to all the same."

He swallowed a couple of times and continued, "I loved your mom so much. She was my first and only love. I never thought she'd die so young and in such a hideous way. Watching you watch her as the tumor took over and finally killed her was the hardest thing I've ever had to go through. I blamed God. I still do, but that's not why I checked out as you put it yesterday. I checked out because it was easier. If I was numb, it didn't hurt so much. I didn't see myself as necessary in your life. You had your friends, your football. What did you need me for? I took the easy way out and for that, I am truly sorry." His voice broke. I watched as tears began to slide down his cheeks.

"Dad." I whispered, "I will always need you. You're my dad."

"Oh, son." He crumpled on the table sobbing.

I got up and did something that a week ago I would never have done. I knelt beside his chair and put my arms around him. "I love you Dad."

He moved and wrapped me in his arms. "I love you too, Ethan. I really do. Can you forgive me?"

"Done." I murmured against his shoulder. "Just promise me you won't shut me out anymore. I loved mom, too. I'm just as guilty as you, it was easier to be angry and let that anger control my life. But, Dad, it almost destroyed me. I don't want that to happen to you, to us."

I pulled back and looked him in the eye. "Mom would want us to live good lives. She would be so mad at both of us right now."

He snorted and wiped his eyes. "You are right about that."

I stood up. "Let's do better. We are all we've got, let's make it count for something."

He nodded and got to his feet too. "I like the sound of that."

"Cool." I nodded my head. I walked back around the table and grabbed my backpack, "I better get to school. I'm going to be late."

"Okay." He patted my back. "Thank you, Ethan. You're a good son."

I drew in a deep breath. "I don't know about that Dad. I may have to do something you aren't going to like today."

"Is it about Emma?" I nodded. He patted my back again. "You do what you need to, son. I won't interfere. Sometimes being a man means owning up to your mistakes. You don't have to worry about any judgment from me. I'm not going anywhere."

"Thank you, Dad." I held up my fist. "To new beginnings."

He bumped his fist against mine. "To new beginnings."

I walked out the kitchen door to my truck feeling about a hundred pounds lighter.

CHAPTER TEN

I arrived at school with a smile on my face. I parked my truck and jumped out. I felt like I was seeing the school for the first time. Everything looked brighter and shinier than I remembered. I hefted my backpack on my shoulder and started toward the side entrance.

As I approached I saw Tommy and Louis. They were shoving someone and laughing. A knot formed in my stomach. They were obviously picking on someone. I sucked in a big breath of air, it was now or never. Was I truly changed?

"Hey guys, what's going on?" I asked as I walked up on the group. My eyes flew open wide. They were picking on Danny.

He wouldn't look at me. I looked at Tommy and Louis. Louis shoved Danny and laughed, "Just getting him warmed up for you, Ethan."

"Yeah, we thought we'd give you something to get your Monday off to a good start," Tommy chimed in. "What happened to you this weekend? You disappeared."

I stepped between Danny and Tommy and Louis and held my hands up. "Knock it off, guys. Leave him alone. He hasn't done anything to you."

"What?" They chimed in chorus. Louis' eyebrows shot straight up. "Dude, what did you do with, Ethan? And who is this sap?"

"Yeah, you can't be Ethan Morgan. It's mandatory he torments Donny at least once a week."

I rolled my eyes. "Cut the crap. You know it's me. And his name is Danny." I pointed at Danny. "And, he's my friend. I'm done picking on other kids. Leave him be."

Tommy threw his hands up, "Whatever you say, man."

Louis wasn't so easily deterred. "Not cool, man. You've practically forced us to pick on everyone in this place for the last four years. Now all of a sudden your favorite target is off limits?"

"No, not just my favorite target, but the entire student body." I raised my hands up in the air. "Who are we to make everyone miserable? I'm sorry I ever thought that was cool or fun."

"Are you on new medication?"

"Yeah, or are you having another seizure?"

"I never had a seizure. I'm fine and I know what I'm doing. I accepted Jesus as my savior. I'm done hurting people."

"You did what?" Tommy chirped.

"You're a Jesus freak?" Louis quipped.

"Call me whatever you want, but I don't want any part of bullying anymore." I turned to Danny. "Come on Danny, let's get to class."

He picked up his book bag and followed me. We walked away from the guys. They just stood and watched us go with their mouths hanging open.

....

Third period came way too fast. I was not looking forward to my talk with Ava. I tapped my pen against the desk, tap, tap…tap, tap, tap…tap, tap until Mr. Hollis glared at me over his glasses. Thankfully the bell rang before he could really let me have it. I jumped up and scooted out the door.

I stopped long enough to throw my books in my locker and grab my jacket. Then I walked quickly down the hall and out one of the side doors. The air was cold and crisp, tree leaves swirled in the wind falling to the ground around me. I drew in a deep breath and forced my muscles to relax. I had known today was going to be hard. I just hadn't realized how draining it was going to be and it was only 10:00a.m.

I crossed the school yard to the football field. I could see Ava sitting in the bleachers. This wasn't the first time we'd skipped out on a class to meet in private, but it was the first time we did it so we could "talk". We usually had more physical needs on our minds.

I jogged up the steps of the bleachers and plopped down beside her. She gave me a weak smile. "Hey."

"Hey yourself."

Her eyes studied my face. "You look tired."

I smiled at her, "I'm exhausted, but I feel better than I have in years."

"Seriously?"

"Seriously."

We started to speak at the same time so I held my hand up and insisted, "You first Ava. What's on your mind?"

She bit her bottom lip and looked away from me to gaze out over the football field. "I thought we should talk about what happened last week."

"I think we have more than Friday night to talk about, don't you?"

Her eyes swept back to mine, "I guess we do." She sighed, "What happened to us Ethan?"

I shoved my hands in the pockets of my jacket and hunched forward. I wasn't really cold, but I couldn't stop shaking. "I've been a total jerk."

She nodded her head acknowledging my statement. "You've been pretty moody lately."

"That's putting it politely." I laughed. "I've been angry and bitter for so long I've forgotten how to have a real relationship with anybody."

I angled my body toward Ava. "I've changed, Ava. After everything that happened with Emma last week, I realize how lost I've become. I'm really sorry I scared you Friday night. I wanted to feel loved, but it was wrong to push you."

"I was afraid you wouldn't stop." She whispered looking away from me.

"I know. I'm glad I came to my senses. Even at my worst I'm not the guy who forces himself on anyone. I was hurt because I knew, know, you don't feel the same about me as you used too."

"Ethan…"

I held up my hand. "You don't have to tell me what you think I want to hear. I get it. I lost my charm a while ago. I wouldn't want to be with me either."

"Oh, Ethan." She sighed. "We used to have a lot of fun, but it was always at someone else's expense. I don't want to be like that anymore."

"Me neither." I shook my head. "I'm a new person. Or, at least I'm trying to be a new person. I accepted Jesus as my savior this weekend."

"You did what?"

"I gave my life to Jesus. I realize now how lost and broken I was and that all my anger was a cry for help. I wish I'd realized it sooner."

Ava cleared her throat. "What do you mean by that?"

I sighed, "Let's just say I wish I would have had my, 'a-ha moment' before Emma got hurt. Unfortunately for her it was her accident that has completely changed my life."

Ava stood up and climbed the last couple of rows of bleachers and leaned against the railing. I stood up and followed her.

She glanced at me; her eyes filled with sorrow. "Ethan, I'm not sure I can get past all of this. I'm glad you've seen the error of your ways, but I don't know if I believe you."

I shrugged. "I know. Time will tell. I don't expect you to forgive me this instant. I agreed to talk to you so we could end things on a friendly note. We've been together a long time, but I don't think we're right for each other anymore."

"Three years." She confirmed. "We've been together since Christmas our freshman year. You asked me to the winter dance."

"And you said 'yes'." I smiled at the memory. "You wore a red dress and your hair in a fancy ponytail. You were beautiful."

"And you were handsome in your suit. I remember when you dropped me off at home and kissed me goodnight. I thought you hung the moon."

"I wish the magic of that night had lasted."

"But it didn't."

"No, it didn't." We've stayed together because you were afraid of what I'd do to your reputation."

"Not an invalid concern."

"True. I would've decimated you and made everyone treat you like you didn't exist."

"And they would have because you are Ethan Morgan, football star, and school big shot."

"Well not anymore. I don't want those things at the cost of everyone around me. I love football but there are way more important things in this life. One of them is finding out what God wants me to do. I want you to know that I want you to be happy and I won't stand in your way or make your life miserable if you find someone new. I'm not going to undermine your position as a cheerleader or make everyone hate you. I'm done with all of that."

She turned her face up to me. "Are you sure? I've seen first-hand what you are capable of doing when you feel betrayed."

"I'm sure." I reached my hand out and pushed her hair out of her face and tucked it behind her ear. "I know it's too soon, but maybe once some time has passed and you've seen this change is for real and I'm different you'll want to give me a second chance."

"Ethan…" Her hand caught mine. She lowered it away from her face.

"Or maybe you won't." I shrugged. " Either way, I would like for us to stay friends. I would love to talk to you about everything that's happened this past week."

She squeezed my hand, "I think I'd like that very much."

....

As soon as school let out I rushed over to the hospital. This time, even though I wanted to see Emma, it was for a different reason. I couldn't wait to tell her I'd gotten saved. My biggest hope was that she would wake up and I could tell her face-to-face.

I swung my truck into a parking spot, jumped out, and jogged toward the hospital. I waved at Millie and headed straight for the elevators. As soon as the doors opened on the second floor, I bolted from the elevator and over to the phone on the wall, picked up the receiver, and dialed the attendant.

The nurse buzzed me through. I yanked open the door and made my way down the hall toward Emma's room. I got to her room and stopped. Danny sat by her bed. He looked up when I stopped in the doorway and smiled.

"Hey Ethan, come on in."

I stepped inside. "Are you sure?"

"Yeah. Come in."

I looked over at Emma. The swelling had gone down a bit, but her bruises looked worse. They were deep purple edged in yellow. The breathing tube was gone. I looked at Danny. "Where's the tube?"

"They took it out this morning. She's breathing on her own."

"Is she awake?"

He shook his head, "No. She's still in a coma. The nurse said it's a good sign that they were able to take the ventilator off, but she couldn't tell me if she'd wake up or not."

I pulled a chair up on the other side of her bed and sat on the edge of the seat. My heart pounded in my chest as I reached for her hand. I don't know what I expected, but it surprised me how warm she felt.

I gripped her small hand in mine and leaned forward. "Hi, Emma. It's Ethan." I fumbled to find words to say. Talking to someone in a coma is awkward.

I kept talking. "I was here the other day, but didn't come in. You look better today. I came by to let you to know I'm really sorry about what happened the other night. You need to wake up so you can yell at me and I can tell you about your visits. I have a feeling you're gonna love that part of this whole mess." I paused and gathered my thoughts before I continued. "I know my apology doesn't erase what I did, but Emma, I am truly sorry to the bottom of my soul. I gave my life to Jesus yesterday. You played a huge role in my decision. So did Danny. I hope when you wake up I can prove to you that I've changed."

I looked over at Danny, "When I leave here, I'm going to the police station."

"What? Why? Are you sure that's a good idea?"

"I have to tell them what really happened. It's not fair that I get away with what I did."

"But, Ethan, you could get in big trouble. Jail time and everything."

I shrugged, "Maybe I belong in jail. Whatever my punishment is, I'll deal with it. I need to do this Danny. I need to make things right."

"It's your call, but I don't think Emma would want you to go to jail."

I squeezed her hand, "Then she needs to wake up and tell me that."

She squeezed my hand back! I jumped up out of the chair.

"Danny, she just squeezed my hand!!!"

He jumped up too. "What?"

"She just squeezed my hand. Emma, can you hear us? If you can, squeeze again."

She squeezed again! I felt tears start to flow down my cheeks.

Danny grabbed her other hand. "Emma, its Danny. I'm here too." He jumped a little. "Oh my God, she squeezed mine too."

We both started laughing and crying at the same time. I leaned closer to her and whispered in a voice that was far from steady. "Keep fighting, Emma. You're almost back. "

"Should I get the doctor?"

I nodded. Danny ran out into the hallway to get a nurse. I smoothed Emma's hair. "You can do this. Come back, Emma. We need you. I need you."

Several nurses flooded into the room followed by a doctor. They ushered us out into the hallway. Danny could barely contain himself. "Ethan, she responded to us! That has to be a good sign."

I nodded in agreement, "Seems like it should be a very good thing."

"This is so awesome. I knew she'd wake up."

I sagged against the wall and put my head in my hands. Tears coursed down my cheeks. "I had my doubts, Danny. I wasn't so sure."

He put his hand on my shoulder. "She's in God's hands, Ethan. She's coming back, I just know it."

"Well, I think I'll head over to the police station and get this over with."

Danny put his hand on my arm, "You sure about this, Ethan?"

"Yeah, I need to make things right. Plus, I don't need to be the first person she sees when she wakes up. She'll want to see you and her family, not the jerk who put her in that bed. I really feel like turning myself in is the right thing to do."

"Ok. I get it." Danny kept his hand on my arm. "Can we pray before you go?"

"Sure."

He bowed his head so I did too. "Dear Lord, we come to you and thank you for letting Emma respond to us. We know in your word it says where two or three are gathered in your name, you are there in the midst of them. Lord, we ask that you stay with Emma and help her come back to us. We know you can do all things. We also ask that you would be with Ethan as he confesses to what happened. We pray you would let the punishment fit the crime and that the judge would see the change in Ethan and keep that in mind. Most importantly Lord, I pray that you will stay by Ethan's side throughout this ordeal and help him grow in your ways and feel your love. In Jesus name, amen."

I wiped away tears and smiled faintly at Danny. "Thank you."

He smiled back at me and then grabbed me in a big hug. This time I didn't freeze. I hugged him back as hard as I could. When we stepped apart, I knew I had found a new friend for life. Danny gave a nod toward me and turned back to Emma's room. I turned and walked back down the hall, out of the ICU, and toward my fate.

....

Emma stood outside on the doorstep of a small coffee shop. She lifted her face to feel the warmth of the sun. The warmth seeped through her entire body. It was so peaceful here. She felt as if she were wrapped in a warm blanket. People moved around her on the street. A young girl walked by clutching a bunny in her arms. She was grinning from ear to ear. An older man sat on a bench across the street reading a newspaper. He looked up and winked at her. She smiled at him. She knew what she'd come here to do, but it was a lot harder than she'd anticipated.

It would be so easy to stay here and join all these happy people. No one was sad, no one seemed hurried, and they all moved along at their own pace. Taking a deep breath to calm her nerves, she put her hand on the door knob and turned.

The tinkling of bells above the door announced her arrival. She looked around the shop and saw the man from the library sitting in the corner by the window. He sat hunched over a laptop sipping coffee.

She made her way through the crowd to His table. "Good morning."

"Emma!" He exclaimed, His entire face lighting up in delight. "Please, have a seat." He motioned the empty chair across from Him.

Emma sank down onto the seat. It was weird to sit with Him knowing who He was. Her eyes roamed His face. He was handsome for sure, but there was more to Him than His looks. Peace radiated from Him in soft waves. She watched silently as His hands flew across the keyboard in sure, swift strokes. He typed a few more words, nodded His head, and then reached up and shut the laptop. He turned His gaze to her. "How are you?"

She smiled a big smile at Him. It was hard not to. His eyes were so warm and inviting. She could feel just how much He cared about her answer by the way His eyes held hers. "It worked!"

He clapped his hands together. "I know! I was so happy when He called out to me last night. I'm getting to know him again and it's wonderful. Emma, you did a great job witnessing to him. How did that feel?"

"Amazing. I was afraid it wasn't going to work. He's very stubborn."

He nodded, "Yes, he is. But you kept at it, even when things looked bleak. We're all so proud of you."

Emma blushed. "I just did what I felt led to do."

"Exactly! Do you know how hard that is for most people?" He reached over and grabbed her hand. Emma felt electricity surge through her entire body. His eyes locked on hers, His voice was soft when He spoke, "Well, the five days are up. Have you considered what should happen now?"

"What do you mean?" she asked startled.

"Do you want to go back and live your physical life? Or, do you want to go with me to Heaven?"

"I get to choose?"

He nodded.

"How do I know which one is the right choice?" Emma gulped and looked out the window of the café. They could've been in any city in the world. There were people milling about, some were obviously in a hurry, some were lounging at tables at the outside café. Another guy walked a very large dog and carried a newspaper tucked under his arm. The biggest difference in this place was that everyone looked peaceful. They moved with purpose, but not with stress and anger. She could definitely get used to living here.

She sighed. "This past week has been pretty incredible. I wouldn't mind staying with you and being finished on earth."

"I sense a but…" He prompted.

She blinked back tears. "There is a but. As much as I would love to become part of Heaven, I don't feel like I'm done on earth. I would love to keep witnessing and bringing more people to you. It seems kind of selfish to stop now."

"I see." He smiled at her, "And, you're ready to go back and see where this new path takes your friends?"

"Yeah, I think so. I mean, you aren't going anywhere right?"

He winked at her, "You got that right."

"So whether I get another day or another fifty years, when I die, I'll see you again."

"Absolutely."

She paused for a minute. She traced the outline on the tablecloth with her finger, after several quiet moments she looked back up and spoke, "Then I think I'd like to go back."

He folded his hands under his chin. His eyes sparkled with joy. "Emma, I am very proud of you."

She blushed. He laughed. "I mean it. Not everyone would have done what you did this past week. You gave a lot of yourself to witness to someone in need. The toll that's taken on your body has been tremendous. In fact, in all reality, you shouldn't get better."

"What?"

"Your injuries were extremely severe. You're breathing was compromised and you had a pretty nasty head trauma. A lot of people wouldn't be able to fight back from the severity of your issues."

"But you can do all things! It says so in the bible."

A smiled spread across His face, "Indeed I can. And, your faith is exactly why you are going to wake up and be fine. Other than being sore and needing time to heal you won't have any lasting effects from the accident. However, there is a catch."

"What's that?"

His eyes grew sad. "You won't remember most of what happened this past week."

Her face fell. "I won't remember the library? My visits to Ethan? You?"

"You'll remember pieces."

Tears filled her eyes. "Will I remember you?"

He reached out and brushed the tears off her cheek. "Not this vividly, no. You'll remember all of this like a dream, a piece here, a piece there. It will feel like a vague memory. But, you will remember the difference you made in two young men's lives. Because of what you sacrificed, they have gotten second chances to get things right."

Emma squared her shoulders. "Then I guess it's worth it. I know your real and no one can ever take that from me."

He smiled at her. "I like you spirit, Emma. You are going to make an amazing missionary.

"Missionary?"

"Yep. Missionary. You are going to travel all over the world and throughout the United States to teach others about me. And you won't be alone."

"Who will be with me?"

"Ahh, I can't reveal that just yet. It would take all the fun out of you discovering your path. All you need to remember is that I'll be there and so will the people you love." He raised his coffee cup. "Here's to the next time we see each other."

At some point in the conversation, a second coffee cup had appeared on the table. Emma picked it up and bumped her cup against his, "Until then…"

……..

Danny was standing in the hallway when a doctor ran by and entered Emma's room. Unable to take the suspense, Danny peeked into the room. There were several nurses and doctors around her bed. He could hear mumblings like, "There's no way this could have happened."

"I can't believe this. She shouldn't have gotten better. Her injuries were too severe."

"Yet, here we are." The doctor exclaimed running a pen light over Emma's eyes. "She's off the ventilator and her pupils are responding to light."

"It's a miracle." one of the nurses whispered.

"Indeed. I can't medically explain her recovery, but it seems she's coming back."

Danny craned his neck to see what was happening. One of the nurses moved and Danny could see Emma's face. Her right eye fluttered open. She blinked several times and looked at the doctors and nurses.

She was awake. Tears filled Danny's eyes as he realized she was finally back!

·······

I parked my truck in an open slot at the police station. I sat and stared at the building for several minutes. Whatever came next was going to change my life.

I chuckled, hadn't my life already changed pretty radically? I'd gone from an angry bully to believing in Jesus and accepting him as my savior. Confessing to what had really happened the night Emma was hurt was the least I could do to give her a little justice.

When she woke up and she had to wake up, I hoped that she would see the changes. However, I wasn't just doing this for her. I was doing it for me. I needed to man up and accept the consequences for my actions. How could I live my life for Jesus with such a big secret? At least now, when my punishment was over, I could dedicate my life to helping other people make the same change I'd made.

I opened the door and climbed out of my truck. I patted the hood and muttered. "Here goes nothing." I walked in the front door, crossed the small lobby and stopped at the reception desk. An older man made his way over to the window. He slid the glass partition open, "Can I help you, son?"

I took a deep breath and answered, "Yes, I need to see Officer Diaz please. It's Ethan Morgan. I have something to tell her about the accident I was in the other night."

EPILOGUE

The room fell silent as Emma made her way to the front of the courtroom and took the stand. She sat down and stared back over the room. The judge turned to face her, "Miss Montgomery, do you understand that you are under oath and required to tell the truth?"

She nodded. "Absolutely."

"Good. Now I understand you want to testify on behalf of Ethan Morgan today?"

"Yes your honor."

"Why would you do that? He has admitted to forcing you off the road and causing you to wreck your bike."

"Yes, your honor."

He threw his hands in air. "I'm at a loss here, can you please explain why in the world you would want to speak up for him?"

Emma smiled at the judge, "I would love to tell you, sir."

He crossed his arms, "Then get on with it. I'm anxious to hear this explanation."

I shifted nervously in my seat. My dad reached over and patted my leg. He gave me a smile that seemed to say 'hang in there'. I looked back at Emma. I couldn't believe six weeks earlier she'd been in a hospital bed fighting for her life because of me. Today, other than the scar on her forehead, you would never know she'd been so close to death. She'd made a remarkable recovery, one that even had her doctors shaking their heads.

I watched her adjust her skirt and start her testimony. My heart flooded with gratitude as she spoke. "Your honor, Ethan Morgan was a bully and a total jerk. If you interviewed all the kids from our school they would tell you some pretty horrible things. Six weeks ago, I would have let you throw the book at him, but that was before everything that happened. Now, Ethan Morgan is a different person. A new person. He gave his life to Jesus, he has accepted the consequences for what he did, and he has worked every day of the last six weeks to make amends to the people he hurt. If you look out over the courtroom, you'll see a lot of his former targets are here to support him."

She motioned to the rows behind me that were filled with kids I'd tormented in one way or another. They'd all made it a point to be here today to support me. Their ability to forgive me has been humbling, to say the least.

Emma continued. "The pastor of our church is here." She pointed to Jason. "He believes Ethan's change is genuine. I believe that too. Yes, he caused me to wreck my bike, but Your Honor, I've forgiven him. I know what the power of Jesus can do in your life. I've seen it first-hand. Ethan spent a lot of years being angry. When he accepted Jesus, that anger went away. Is he perfect? No. Is he genuinely trying to live for God? Yes. I would like to ask you, Your Honor, to take that into consideration when you declare his sentence. Ethan doesn't need prison or jail. He needs the chance to continue his relationship with Jesus. There is no better disciplinarian than God."

The judge sat speechless for a few minutes. He cleared his throat. "Thank you, Miss Montgomery. Your testimony was powerful and well said. However, in light of what Mr. Morgan did, I'm not sure I can absolve him. He hurt you, very nearly killed you. I can't let that go unpunished. I need some time to consider everything that's been said today." He banged the gavel and stood up, "Courts in recess for thirty minutes while I ponder what to do with you, Mr. Morgan." He gave me a very pointed look and walked out one of the side doors.

I sank down in my chair. It didn't look good. Danny came up from one of the back rows and patted my shoulder. "Hang in there, Ethan. He'll see reason."

"Yeah, Ethan. He'll see that you've changed." Tommy piped in. Surprisingly after my change, Tommy and I have gotten to be even better friends. He was eager to embrace the new me and stop all the hazing and bullying.

Jason reached over and squeezed my shoulder. "We're here for you, no matter what happens. God can do all things, even soften a judge's heart. Don't get defeated."

I smiled. "I'm not. I'm at peace with whatever happens. I know even if I'm in a prison cell, I won't be alone."

My dad cleared his throat and looked away. I grabbed his hand. "Dad, you okay?"

He turned and looked back at me, his eyes were misty with tears. "I'm just really proud of you Ethan, at how your handling all this. Your mom would be too."

I blinked back tears. "Thanks Dad."

....

A few minutes later, the door behind the judge's bench swung open and the bailiff called out, "All rise."

I got to my feet and wiped my sweaty palms on my pants. My entire body shook with anticipation. The judge made his way in and sat down. He opened and shut my file several times. Taking his glasses off, he rubbed his eyes and then looked out over the courtroom. His eyes landed on me and locked onto mine.

"Young man, I've come to a decision. This wasn't easy and shouldn't be taken lightly. You almost killed a wonderful young woman. A young woman who is here today and, to my utter amazement, has begged for mercy on your behalf. I sincerely hope what she said is true. I hope you've found a way to change your life and turn it into something positive." He waved his gavel over the crowd. "There certainly are a lot of people willing to give you a second chance. The question is, should the court give you a second chance?"

He pinched his nose between his fingers and blew out a big breath. "Ethan Morgan, the court finds you guilty of assault. Your punishment is to serve eight hundred hours of community service. I do not feel jail time would benefit you. I am assigning you to the Oakdale boys home where you will live on the weekends, teach the boys football, and mentor them on the consequences of bullying. They could use a good influence and I think you, along with your friends, could guide them down a better road than you've travelled."

His eyes locked back on mine. "If at any point, I hear of any instances that you have gone back to your old ways, you will serve the remainder of your sentence in the adult county jail. Do you understand your sentence Mr. Morgan?"

I wobbled on legs of jelly as the reality of my sentence hit me. I nodded my head. "Your Honor, I would be honored to help at the boy's home. Thank you."

He glared at me over his glasses as he perched them back on his nose. "Don't disappoint me, son. I don't want to see you in this courtroom again. Dismissed." He banged the gavel.

I slumped down in my chair as tears of relief flowed down my cheeks. I could hear the cheering behind me as my friends all joined in celebrating the fact I wasn't headed to jail.

I felt a hand on my shoulder and looked up. Emma's smile lit up the room. "This is awesome. Ethan, you can pay forward the grace you were given to all those boys. Just think about what Jesus can do with eight hundred hours!"

To learn more about the authors, please visit:

www.JulieandMitchKelly.com

Made in the USA
Columbia, SC
19 December 2023